He held out his hand formally. "I'm Wyndy Sarto," he said.

"You're Wendy?" I asked, dumbfounded. I looked at him with dismay. He wasn't going to do at all! Not only was he a boy, but he was not the right kind of boy. I didn't know what was the more off-putting, his calm self-possession, or the way he

looked. He had the smoothest dark hair I'd ever seen curving over his ears just to the nape of his neck. His skin was fair, but his well-defined eyebrows were dark, his lashes were dark, and the lids of his eyes were the dusky color of the true brunette. His clothes were crisp perfection. From the casual white linen suit to his rope-soled canvas shoes, there was neither a smudge nor wrinkle to show that he'd been on the plane for more than ten hours....

Dear Readers:

Thank you for your unflagging interest in First Love From Silhouette. Your many helpful letters have shown us that you have appreciated growing and stretching with us, and that you demand more from your reading than happy endings and conventional love stories. In the months to come we will make sure that our stories go on providing the variety you have come to expect from us. We think you will enjoy our unusual plot twists and unpredictable characters who will surprise and delight you without straying too far from the concerns that are very much part of all our daily lives.

We hope you will continue to share with us your ideas about how to keep our books your very First Loves. We depend on you to keep us on our toes!

Nancy Jackson
Senior Editor
FIRST LOVE FROM SILHOUETTE

WITH LOVE
FROM ROME
Janice Harrell

First Love from Silhouette

Published by Silhouette Books New York

America's Publisher of Contemporary Romance

SILHOUETTE BOOKS
300 E. 42nd St., New York, N.Y. 10017

ISBN: 0-373-06205-2

First Silhouette Books printing October 1986

America's Publisher of Contemporary Romance

Printed in the U.S.A.

RL 6.4, IL age 11 and up

First Love from Silhouette by Janice Harrell

JANICE HARRELL is the eldest of five children and spent her high-school years in the small central Florida town of Ocala. She earned her B.A. at Eckerd College and her M.A. and Ph.D from the University of Florida. For a number of years she taught English at the college level. She now lives with her husband and their young daughter.

Chapter One

The day it all began I was over at my friend Audrey's house watching her thumbtack feminist slogans to the bulletin board in her room. The first one had said in bold purple letters, "Adam was a rough draft." Now she was pinning up a long orange one that said, "Whatever women do they must do twice as well as men to be thought half as good. Luckily, this is not difficult."

I didn't go along with Audrey's view a hundred percent. I saw that boys were the weaker sex, but that was all the more reason for us to go out of our way to help them. Nice but help-less—that was the way I would have summed them up. I couldn't know then that in the days to come my point of view was going to take a sharp turn around.

I stretched out on one of the twin beds and wiggled my bare toes. Maybe I should put fresh polish on my toenails before school started. It wouldn't do to begin the school year with chipped polish. But I could put off doing that for a few more days. There were just a few of the lovely, lazy days of summer left, and I wanted to spend them enjoying myself. I did not want to paint my toenails and I did not want to get sucked into a hot discussion about the oppression of women, either. Too tiring.

When Audrey pinned up the third slogan, though, I forgot that I was determined not to get into an argument. "A woman needs a man like a fish needs a bicycle," it said. I couldn't help speaking up.

"Wait a minute," I said. "You're going too far, there. I like having boys around. Who would want to live in a world without any boys?"

"Me," said Audrey, sticking in another thumbtack. "It would be a nice change."

Then she turned and looked seriously at me. Audrey could look very impressive when she got serious. I am a small, shrimpy type with ordinary brown hair and could never overawe anybody, but Audrey is a tall blonde with flashing eyes. When she drew herself up to her full height she could have been one of those Nordic goddesses who went around hurling thunderbolts when they got annoyed. I stirred uneasily. I did not really expect her to hurl a thunderbolt, but it was clear that something was brewing.

"I've got to tell you something, Jess," she said. "I'm going away to school this year."

"What!" I screeched, sitting bolt upright. "How can you be going away to school?"

"Don't you remember last spring when Mom and Dad took me to look at girls' schools?"

"Sure, I remember. But you applied too late to get in. You told me that."

"I got put on the waiting list. Now my name has come up. Chowan Hall called us this morning."

"How can you do this to me?" I wailed. "I'll be all alone over there at Senior High. Everybody knows they eat sophomores for breakfast at that place. Who am I going to *talk* to?"

"I'll be in the same shape. I'm not going to know a soul at Chowan."

"So don't go! What's wrong with Senior High?"

"I'll have a lot more opportunities at Chowan. I'll have a good shot at a class office there. The most I'll ever get elected to at Senior High is secretary of something or other. Between the girls who vote for boys just because they're good-looking and the boys who won't vote for girls no matter what, I don't have a chance of being elected to anything around here," she said, a tinge of bitterness in her voice.

I knew that Audrey had been upset when she lost out on president of the Freshman Class to dopey Steve Futtrell, but I hadn't thought it would come to this.

"It's going to be a terrible rush to get ready," she went on. "I've got just this week to get everything together and packed. You wouldn't believe all I've got to take with me. Take a look at the list." She reached over to her desk and began rummaging around in a drawer.

I couldn't have cared less about everything Audrey was going to have to cart off to Chowan Hall. What I cared about was that she was deserting me, but suddenly I realized that nothing I could say now was going to make any difference. She was already practically packing her bags to leave. "I guess you're really excited about going," I said in a hollow tone.

"Am I ever!" she said. "I knew you'd understand, Jess. I've been dreading telling you, but I knew you'd see that I need to go someplace where I can spread my wings. Of course, I'm a bit nervous about going away, but I really liked Chowan Hall when we visited the campus. They have a first-rate science lab, these gorgeous playing fields, positively acres of green lawns...."

I was vaguely conscious of Audrey's droning on about the advantages of her new school, but I was too swept over by a wave of despair to take it all in. The two of us had been best friends since the fifth grade. How was I going to get along without her? After all, I was going to be going to a new school, too. Next week we were to begin our first year at Senior High, which was, compared to Johnson Junior High, like the Amazon jungle compared to Friendly Village. I wasn't exactly afraid of moving up to Senior High—at least I wasn't out-and-out terrified—but I had been counting on Audrey's being right there with me for support.

I suppose she must have finally come to the end of the list of the advantages of Chowan Hall because through my fog of depression I heard her say, "Hey, isn't this the day your mom gets back from New York?"

"Oh, my gosh," I said, casting a guilty look at my watch. "She's probably home already. I completely forgot about it." I jumped up and slipped my sandals back on. Mom had gone to New York by herself for a getaway weekend to meet an old friend she hadn't seen in years. I knew her feelings would be hurt if I wasn't even home to meet her when she got in.

"Well, you don't have to look so gloomy," said Audrey as she walked with me to the door. "We can write to each other, you know. And I'll be home for Thanksgiving."

Great. Thanksgiving was months away.

"You're going to get along just fine without me," she went on. "If you think about it, with the two of us, it's always been you that's been the doer. I just follow your lead more often than not."

"Is that why you decided to go away to school? You think I'm too bossy?"

"Don't be dumb," she said. "I'm just saying it doesn't make sense to act as if you're going to be lost without me when half the time I'm just your cheering section. Who was it who convinced Mrs. Bradford she was giving us too much homework? Who figured out a way to break Barfy of chasing cars? Who won the ninth grade essay contest?"

"I need moral support," I said glumly.

"You're going to get along great, idiot. Think about me! I'll be completely on my own and I don't have your sneaky, sharp brain."

It was true, I thought with a touch of complacency. I did have a sneaky brain, if I said so myself. I could usually figure out how to get what I wanted one way or another. But then I hadn't been faced before with a major blow like Audrey's leaving me.

"I'll come by tomorrow," I said.

"Not tomorrow. Mom and I have to go to Raleigh to shop. We've got that whole long list of things for me to buy. Come over on Wednesday morning and we'll sew on name tags."

"I can't wait."

I headed home at a half trot, feeling, in spite of all Audrey's reassurance, slightly sick to my stomach. Even the Lone Ranger had Tonto. Who was I going to have? Marian Beasley and I got along okay, but if you told Marian anything personal it was over half the school the next day. Holly Wainwright was a good friend in a pinch, but if I started spending more time with her than I was spending already, I was going to get pretty tired of the way she kept pointing out ways I could improve myself. Karen Harper had the advantage of living right down the street from me, but though she was a nice kid she had no more backbone than a wet noodle. I heaved a large sigh. As I rounded our corner I saw Mom's car in the driveway.

I flung open the front door. "Mom!" I yelled.

She popped out of the kitchen with an apple in her hand. "I had the most wonderful time," she said, hugging me with her free arm. "Did you miss me, sugar?"

"Sure."

She grinned. "Liar. I called Dad and told him to bring home Chinese food. I'm starving."

Just then I heard the crunch of Dad's car on the gravel of the driveway. "Here he is now," said Mom. "I hope he remembered the egg rolls."

"Mom, Audrey's going away to school!" I said. "She's going to Chowan Hall and she won't be home until Thanksgiving. Isn't that awful? I can't believe this is happening to me!"

"Well, they have been talking about her going to boarding school for some time, dear."

"I never thought she'd really do it, though," I said.

Mom opened the door for Dad as he was holding three white paper sacks, one of which had already begun to drip.

"I think I tipped over the moo goo gai pan," he said. "It's starting to leak."

"Give it here," said Mom.

He handed her a paper sack and bent to peck her on the cheek. "Did you have a good time?" he asked, following her to the kitchen.

"Fantastic! Sally and I had lunch at the Plaza on Saturday. I've decided I like luxury."

I was left in the front hall. Nobody but me really appreciated what a disaster Audrey's leaving was. Finally, I trailed into the kitchen. Maybe my fortune cookie would have some good advice to offer.

Mom was unpacking the paper bags. "Oh, you remembered to ask for extra duck sauce. Good. Jess, would you put some ice in the glasses?"

It struck me that my parents were a callous lot. They both seemed to be in terrific moods. The gloom that had settled over me was like an individual, isolated black cloud. I put ice in the glasses, then while Mom and Dad unpacked all the bags I broke open my fortune cookie. "You are the luckiest of the lucky," it said. I had seldom run into a fortune cookie that was more off the mark. It was disgusting.

Mom seemed to have completely forgotten about me and my problems. She was already deep in telling Dad about her trip to New York. "Sally hasn't aged a day," she burbled. "And the glamorous life she's had you wouldn't believe. She's been to Egypt and seen the pyramids, she's been shopping in Hong Kong and taken a cruise around the Greek islands. And they've lived . . . oh, all over. I forget all the places."

"What does her husband do for a living?" Dad asked. Deftly he cut open a plastic packet of duck sauce with the kitchen scissors.

"I'm not sure her husband works at all," said Mom. "Maybe he just collects dividends. He's the Sarto of Sarto Motors. Giovanni's great-grandfather was the founder of the company."

"Aren't you glad we don't live shallow, useless lives of pleasure like that?" asked Dad, a humorous glint in his eyes.

"Ye-es," said Mom, not sounding completely convinced. "But really Richard, you've got to admit it sounds like fun, doesn't it? And Sally's just the same as always, so beautiful, so fresh. She has charm. She always has had, you know. It's a way of making you feel you're the most important person in the world. When we got together, the years just fell away." She sighed a little. "It seemed exactly the way it was when we were chums back in Pawtucket."

I tried to imagine Audrey and me meeting at the Plaza for lunch years from now, both of us sleek and sophisticated, talking about our trips around the world and our exciting careers. It didn't cheer me up any. I needed a friend now, not twenty years from now when I would be too old and decrepit to care about anything.

"Does this Sally have any children?" asked Dad.

"No...yes...oh, I'm not sure," said Mom. "It didn't come up. We were so busy talking about old times and things."

"Like Egypt," suggested Dad.

Mom smiled. "You can't blame her for laying it on a little. She's come a long way from Pawtucket, North Carolina."

I stolidly ate my way through my moo goo gai pan, brooding all the time on my bleak future, but unfortunately no one seemed even to notice how miserable I was. When Mom finally finished giving us her point by point account of the trip, I was totally sick of hearing about Sally Sarto and her thrilling life, but at least, I figured, I had heard the last of it. After all, I told myself, it had been twenty years since Sally and Mom last got together. I imagined it would be twenty more until she heard from her again. Little did I know!

Wednesday morning I went over to Audrey's and spent all morning helping her get ready to go off to Chowan Hall. It was amazing how many articles of clothing she was taking with her, not to mention odds and ends like a laundry bag, a shower cap, skis, and her oboe. We must have sewn on hundreds of name tags. "Couldn't we use iron-on name tags?" I asked.

"I'm afraid iron-on tags would come off in the dryer," said Audrey, her needle busily at work. "But you can use marker on things like the shower cap. That will save time. You know, Jess, the beauty of going to an all-girls school is that people there aren't going to be so caught up in clothes and worrying about what they wear. They'll be concentrating on more important things than impressing boys. Nobody's going to feel that they have to act dumb to attract them. Everybody'll be free to concentrate on studies. And then we'll all have so much more opportunity to develop our leadership talents. It's going to be real freedom. I can't wait."

I tried my best to be a good listener while at the same time sewing name tags on handkerchiefs, but by the time we had finished for the morning, I was feeling pretty awful. It hadn't done anything for my spirits to hear Audrey going on as if she were heading off to paradise. After all, I was going to be left in Pine Falls, fighting it out in the real world. I left her house at lunchtime feeling pretty low.

When I got home, Mom was on the phone.

"Can you talk louder, Sally?" she was saying. "This connection is so bad." There was a long silence. Then I heard Mom say, "Well, of course, if you think it would help out, I'd be glad to.... Oh, no, don't worry about it. We've got plenty of room, and as you say it won't be for long.... No, it's no trouble at all, really. We'll drive over and meet the plane. Just give me the arrival time and the flight number." Mom reached for a pencil. "Give that to me again. This connection is terrible." She jotted down some numbers on the pad. "Now don't worry about it. I'm glad to help out. After all, what are friends for?"

When Mom hung up, she looked a little uneasy for a second, but the uneasy look was swiftly washed away by a look that was all too familiar. It was the same look she had when she assured me that we were going to have a wonderful time visiting Auntie Dorothy or that mowing the lawn was fantastic exercise.

"Guess what!" she said. "I've got a lovely surprise for you!"

I didn't think I could stand any more surprises after the one Audrey had sprung on me, but I tried to keep from cringing visibly.

"Wendy Sarto is coming to stay with us for a while!"

"I thought your friend's name was Sally." Then I had an unpleasant thought. "Wait a minute. Is this Wendy, Sally's kid?"

"That's right! And she's just about a year older than you are. Isn't that nice?"

"I'm overcome with delight."

"Darling," said Mom, "I do wish just for once you would approach something new without making a sarcastic remark."

"I could," I said, "but it wouldn't be the same." I sat down and prepared to hear the worst. "All right, tell me about this Wendy person."

"I don't know very much," said Mom. "The transatlantic connection was just terrible."

"How long is she going to stay?"

"I'm not exactly sure. The thing is, Sally has gotten this wonderful chance to go along on Lord Englebrich's expedition to the Himalayas. Naturally, she couldn't pass up a once in a lifetime opportunity."

Dad stepped in the front door. "What's this about a once in a lifetime opportunity? Have we won the lottery or something?"

"No, but Sally Sarto's kid is coming to stay with us," I said, "and Mom says that will be just as nice."

Mom shot me a nasty look. Then she began all over again, telling Dad about the phone call with the bad connection and the Himalayan expedition while he fixed himself a sliced turkey sandwich.

"Doesn't this kid have a father she can stay with?" asked Dad, swabbing mustard over his sandwich. "What about this Giovanni you mentioned?"

Mom looked a little embarrassed. "It seems Giovanni is just right now in a Swiss . . . uh, sanitarium."

"Crazy?" said Dad, looking interested.

"Certainly not," said Mom. "He's just . . . uh, in need of a long rest."

"Oh," said Dad. "A drunk."

"You see, I couldn't very well say no, Richard," Mom said. "And we do have an extra room."

"It's fine with me," said Dad. "I just wonder if Sally has given you the whole story. There must be some kind of school she could put the kid in. After all, money doesn't seem to be a problem."

"Money is *just* the problem," Mom said, lowering her voice. "It seems the poor kid barely escaped a kidnapping attempt a few months ago—right in broad daylight in downtown Rome. I guess with the Sartos being rich they were obvious targets. Anyway, somebody actually pulled a gun on their chauffeur one morning when he was driving Wendy to school. The chauffeur kept his head and stepped on the accelerator hard so the gunman missed and the bullet lodged in the dashboard, but ever since then they've felt as if they had to keep Wendy under heavy guard. Naturally, it's driving the poor kid crazy. Sally thinks it would be better to get her out of Rome entirely, but now with this Himalayan expedition coming up she isn't really in a position to move the entire household just now, so she thought of me. Wendy could stay with us for a while. Then when Sally gets back she'll make some more permanent arrangement."

"Isn't Wendy a kind of funny name for an Italian kid?" I put in.

"I think I got the name right," said Mom, looking uncertain. "Anyway, Wendy's only half Italian."

"Does she speak English?"

"I'm sure she must," said Mom, "with her own mother being an American. I would have liked to get more details, but really the connection was horrible and Sally was in such a rush to go out and get all the things she's going to need for the expedition."

She was probably going to buy name tags, I thought. Audrey, Sally—everybody seemed to be setting off for some great adventure except me. I got to stay at home and welcome Wendy Sarto, and I had my doubts about that whole business. I think I'm as hospitable as the next guy, but I couldn't help wondering why nobody else the Sartos knew had rushed forth to take in darling little Wendy.

I thought a moment. "You know, this kid is probably used to having servants and a big house and all that. Why would she want to come and live in a small town with some perfect strangers?''

"Probably Sally sold her on the idea," said Mom. "When we were in New York, Sally told me that her happiest memories were of her life in small town America. It was idyllic—that's what she said."

"Sure," said Dad. "That's why she went running off to Rome."

"I don't understand why you two are such cynics," said Mom. "I'm not worried at all about Wendy fitting in here. Sally didn't get to say much about her, but I distinctly remember her saying 'Wendy is very adaptable.' "

As the last few days of summer dribbled away and Audrey got more and more impossible to be around with her constant chirruping about Chowan Hall, I began to feel more philosophical about Wendy's arrival. It was clear that I needed a new best friend. Who knows? I thought. Maybe this Wendy can be my friend. Senior High was going to be as new to her as it was to me. Even newer if she'd never lived in the States before. Maybe I could even help her find her way around. I liked helping people out. Look at the way I'd been helping Peter Fields, the boy next door. He was a nice guy but helpless in some ways, and all last year I had stood faithfully by, loading his camera, adjusting his reflectors, and fetching his props while he photographed all the glamour girls of the ninth grade in his backyard. Naturally, I hoped that someday he would look up at me as if out of a daze and say, "Jessica! It was you all the time that I was looking for. You're worth twenty of these cheerleaders." But I wasn't holding my breath.

By the end of the week I was actually looking forward to Wendy's arrival. I had to tell Audrey that I wouldn't be able to come over and see her off Saturday because I was going to have to drive to Raleigh with the folks to meet Wendy's plane.

"I understand," she said. "We can just say goodbye now. Naturally, you need to be there to meet her and make her feel at home. Oh, Jessie," she said, "I'm really going to miss you."

I was startled to see tears in her eyes. Audrey was not the emotional type. "I'll come to see you off tomorrow," I said, alarmed. "Mom and Dad can go pick up Wendy by themselves."

"No," she said, "You need to go meet the plane. You'll be such a help to her." She sniffled. "She'll be lucky to have a friend like you."

"Audrey, you're going to just *love* Chowan Hall."

"I know," she said, in a rather small voice. "But I'm really going to miss you."

As I went home I had plenty of food for thought. If Audrey was falling apart just going over to Chowan Hall in Maryland, poor Wendy must be coming completely unglued to be setting off for a strange country and a strange family thousands of miles away from her parents. I would have to be careful to put her at ease, make her feel at home. Maybe I could do a little reading up on Italy, find out about the country she came from. Probably she was used to a whole different way of doing things. I was going to have to try to be very sensitive to what was going on with her if I meant to be really helpful.

When I got home, I took a critical look at the bedroom across the hall from mine, the spare bedroom. Mom had already taken out the old sewing machine, the outgrown bicycle and the Christmas wrapping paper that had been junking up the place, but still it didn't look exactly homey. I should try to make it look more welcoming. I didn't have much time but I thought I could make some improvement in it, give it that personal touch.

"I'm going to fix up Wendy's room," I called to Mom.

"What a sweet thought," she said, beaming at me. "I knew I could count on you, sugar."

The first thing I did was to rummage around in the attic until I found some white eyelet curtains with ruffles. When I had washed the ruffled curtains and put them up in place of the beige draperies, the place immediately began to look less like a motel room and more like a girl's room. The next morning, I dug up my old pink bedspread. It was still perfectly good. The only reason it was up in the attic was that I had gotten sick of pink. I hung a potpourri in the closet then I lined the drawers and put little satin sachet bags in them. A vase full of zinnias from the garden helped a lot, and once I had put a couple of lacy pillows on the bed I felt the place looked positively inviting. Mom agreed.

"I know Wendy will appreciate all the time and thought you've put into making the room nice," she said. "It's adorable. Now it looks as if it's expecting an honored guest."

I felt satisfied. I hadn't really expected to spend the last few precious moments of my summer vacation rushing around doing housework, but it was in a good cause and besides, it made me feel better. I still felt a little sick whenever I stopped work and realized that Audrey was on her way to Chowan Hall, but I could see that my problems were nothing compared to what Wendy Sarto was up against. Maybe it was true what Mom was always saying, that the best way to forget your troubles was to get involved in helping somebody else.

"When is the plane coming in?" I asked.

"At noon," said Mom. "I just called the airport and they said it was expected to be on time, so we'd better be going soon."

I went to my room to run a brush through my hair, considering as I did whether I should get a body wave or not. I had only considered the question a hundred times or so, my hair needed something, but I wasn't sure a body wave was it.

I found myself hoping Wendy Sarto wasn't going to turn out to be terribly chic and blasé. I didn't need anything to make me feel even more insecure. Then, suddenly a pleasant thought struck me. Weren't Italians supposed to be short and dark? Of course, Wendy was only half Italian, but even if she were only *halfway* short and dark it might be a good thing. Nobody ever had a better friend than Audrey, but there was no denying that my running around with a Nordic goddess type had tended to make me look even shorter and more insignificant than I was already.

"Ready, Jessica?" Dad called from the living room. "We've got to get going."

"Coming," I called.

It took us well over an hour to drive to the airport, and during the whole drive I felt that delightful glow that you feel when you know you've been very good. I'm a pretty nice person, I thought to myself. I'm going to be very sweet to this Wendy Sarto. I might even be willing to lend her some of my clothes.

When we got to the airport, Mom anxiously noted that Flight 137 had arrived. People were already walking down the steps of the plane carrying tote bags and garment bags. Mom peered anxiously out the big plate glass window trying to see who was getting off, but a luggage van and a mail wagon pulled out in front of the window, making it hard to see.

While Mom and Dad strained to get a view of the people getting off the plane, I looked around. The usual assortment of airport types was going past, a businessman in a three-piece suit carrying a teddy bear home to his kid, a harassed mother trying to keep track of three suitcases and four small children.

One guy I couldn't quite place was sitting near us, a dark-haired boy who looked about college age. I knew that most colleges had been in session for over a week so I couldn't figure out where he was going. Maybe he had had a death in the family and had been called home suddenly. The only problem with that theory was that he was dressed like somebody out of *Miami Vice* in a white linen jacket over a peach-colored T-shirt. Somehow the outfit did not suggest funerals.

"I don't understand it," said Mom anxiously. "Everybody's gotten off, and there's no sign of her. Nobody has gotten off that plane that was a day under forty." Suddenly she grabbed Dad's hand. "Oh, what if the kidnappers have got Wendy?" she breathed. "I'll never forgive myself. How will I break it to Sally?"

The dark-haired boy near us looked over at us curiously. I wished Mom would not stand in the middle of the airport talking about kidnappings. I hated for us to make a spectacle of ourselves.

"You probably wrote the flight number down wrong," said Dad. "Or maybe she missed a connection."

To my alarm, the boy was walking over to us, his hands in his pants pockets. Mom's fears had so stirred up my imagination that for a wild second there I expected him to produce a ransom note.

"Excuse me," he said, "but are you the MacAlisters?"

"Yes," said Mom, clinging to Dad.

He held out his hand formally. "I'm Wyndy Sarto," he said.

"*You're* Wendy?" I put in, dumbfounded.

"You were expecting me," said the dark-haired boy.

"Yes, of course, we were," said Dad, clasping his hand. "It's just that we were expecting . . . well . . . a girl."

There was an awkward pause.

"Your mother and I didn't have long to talk," Mom said quickly, "the connection was so bad, and you see in the United States, Wendy is usually a girl's name. You did say your name was Wendy?"

"Wyndham Sarto," he said. He pulled his passport out of his breast coat pocket and silently held it out for Mom and Dad to see.

"Of course," said Mom faintly. "Of course, you're Wyndy. It's just we're so surprised. You don't . . . uh . . . look much like your mother."

"No," he said tranquilly.

I looked at him with dismay. *This* was what I was getting to replace Audrey? He wasn't going to do at all! Not only was he a boy, but he was not the right kind of boy. He was all wrong. I didn't know what was more off-putting, his calm self-possession or the slick perfection of the way he looked. He had the smoothest dark hair I had ever seen curving over his ears and just to the nape of his neck. His skin was fair, but his well-defined eyebrows were dark, his lashes black, and the lids of his eyes were the dusky color of the true brunette. His clothes were crisp perfection. From the casual white linen suit he wore to the rope-soled canvas shoes, there was neither a smudge nor a wrinkle to show that he'd been on the plane over ten hours. There was something faintly inhuman about it.

He caught me staring at him and gave me a cool smile. To my fury, I blushed.

"You haven't picked up your luggage yet, have you?" said Dad.

"No," he said.

"Well, why don't you and Jessica go over and take care of that, and we'll go get a luggage cart," said Dad.

I knew that Dad and Mom wanted to get away a moment to talk about this new development, but I didn't relish being left alone with Wyndham Sarto the perfect. He had a way of making me feel about five years old and totally insignificant. Of course, I reminded myself in all justice, he might imagine I was younger than I really was because of my being slightly on the short side. I would have to figure out some way to work my age into the conversation.

The two of us walked over to the luggage carousel and stood watching oddly assorted luggage snake its way past us while I tried to figure out a casual way of mentioning that I'd be sixteen in a matter of a few months. He had pushed the sleeves of his white jacket up to his elbows and was standing with a foot resting on the steel edge of the carousel. Unfortunately, the casual posture did not diminish his look of perfection. It was intimidating.

Nylon suitcases banded with bright stripes, brightly colored duffel bags, battered luggage held together with luggage straps went slowly by us. I recognized Wyndy's at once. It made its unsteady jolting way through the curtain of black plastic strips and moved toward us, a trim but opulent-looking soft brown leather case with brass fittings.

He lifted the case off the conveyer belt and set it beside him. Soon another one like it appeared on the carousel. My eyes widened as a third, a fourth, and a fifth matching suitcase made their way toward us. Finally, Wyndy plucked off the conveyer belt a tennis racket and a small alligator hide case.

"Is that all?" I asked.

"Yes," he said. "The rest will be coming by boat."

I could hear Mom's voice approaching us. "We could give him our room," she was murmuring to Dad, "and we could move into the small bedroom. Or maybe we could convert the garage into an apartment. You know, we've talked about that for a long time...." As we turned to face them, her voice trailed off and she smiled brightly at us. It was obvious to me that she was desperately trying to figure out a way to house the perfect Wyndy as far away from her darling daughter as possible.

Mom and Dad were pushing a luggage carrier, but I noticed Dad's eyes opened a trifle when he spotted the vast array of beautiful leather luggage beside us. Probably he was wondering, as I was, what exactly Sally Sarto had meant when she told Mom that Wyndy wouldn't be staying "long."

We piled all the luggage on the wheeled carrier and began pushing it toward the parking lot, with Dad asking polite questions about how the flight had gone and what the weather had been like in Rome, while Mom and I tried to cope with our disordered feelings. One of the things that had thrown us off balance, I realized, was that Wyndy was not just the wrong sex—he looked too grown-up. He was supposedly only a year ahead of me, but it was hard to believe. Partly it was his height, I suppose. He was as tall as Dad. But I think it was also the way he acted. He was too cool by half. It was hard to square this self-possessed young man with the bewildered girl we had expected to meet.

We managed to fit all his suitcases except for one into the trunk of our little Toyota. The extra one was wedged between Wyndy and me on the back seat. The tennis racket was put at my feet since I obviously had the shortest legs. We had to make conversation all the way home, and it was clear as we talked, rather stiffly, that no one was really comfortable.

"Is this your first visit to the U.S.?" asked Dad as we drove out of the airport parking lot.

"I used to come pretty often to visit my grandparents," he said.

I looked at him sharply, wondering why he hadn't gone to stay with them this time. As if reading my mind, he added smoothly, "Before they died, that is."

"Ah, yes," said Dad. "You're half American."

"Dual citizenship," said Wyndy, "until I'm eighteen."

In fact, he had no trace of an Italian accent. His pronunciation was a little too careful and controlled to be quite homegrown, but he definitely had an American accent.

"I suppose your mother must be winging her way to Nepal by now," Dad said.

"Yes," Mom put in, "I had no idea Sally was so interested in mountain climbing."

"I think she's more interested in becoming Lady Engle-brich," said Wyndy.

"But she's already married!" I exclaimed involuntarily.

He looked at me as if I were not very bright. "That could be fixed," he said.

I could tell Mom was not too happy with the direction the conversation was taking. "She's done some mountain climbing before, though, hasn't she?" she asked hastily.

"Yes," he said. "It's a crazy hobby—as I've mentioned to her once or twice."

"It can be dangerous," Mom acknowledged. "I guess you can't help but worry about her."

He shrugged. "It's not that. After all, you can get killed easily enough just crossing the street. I don't see the point in it, that's all. The cold, the work, the lousy food. It's the kind of thing Sal likes, though, because it's good for bragging about after it's over."

I was momentarily jolted by Wyndy's calling his mother by her first name, though I supposed I should have guessed he would from the way he talked about her as if she were his stupid sister instead of his mother.

"Maybe she likes it," I suggested. "I think I'd like mountain climbing. It sounds terrifically exciting."

"I don't think you would," he said. "It's pretty uncomfortable."

"Maybe you didn't realize it, Wyndy," Dad interjected, "but school starts day after tomorrow. You're going to be a junior, is that right?"

"I guess so."

"You might find an American high school a bit of a switch from what you're used to," said Dad.

"I did go to an American school in Rome," Wyndy offered. "Sally's always had it in mind for me to go to an American college. That's why."

Mom had obviously been brooding over the problem of his entering Senior High using a girl's name because she turned back toward him as we sped down the highway and said, "Have you ever thought of using your middle name while you're living in the U.S.?''

He looked puzzled for an instant and Mom decided he wasn't sure what a middle name was. "For example," she added kindly, "my name is Susan Mary MacAlister, so Mary is my middle name. I call myself Susan, but I could just as easily call myself Mary."

His brow cleared. "I have two middle names," he said, "Giuseppi and Andrea. Which one do you think would work out best?"

Mom blinked. "Of course, you're *used* to Wyndy so maybe you'd like to stick with that," she said quickly.

I suspected that Wyndy was secretly smiling at Mom. There wasn't the slightest tremor of his lips, but his eyes became slightly triangular the way people's do when they roar with laughter. I stole a curious glance at him. This was probably what was meant, I realized, by having "laughing eyes." He then unbent enough to say, "Don't worry about it, Mrs. MacAlister. I don't think people bother about your name once they get to know you. But I'll introduce myself as Wyndham if it'll make you feel better."

"I didn't mean . . ." said Mom. "Of course . . ."

Wyndy's eyes crinkled again.

Dad cleared his throat. I was beginning to think Wyndy made my parents as uncomfortable as he made me.

I stole a glance at Wyndy's white linen suit and began to wonder if Pine Falls, North Carolina was quite ready for Wyndham Giuseppi Andrea Sarto. Pine Falls was not exactly a small town; it was more a small city. But it still had a small-town flavor. Not only was it a pretty conservative place in general but when it came to clothes it was, to put it mildly, not in the forefront of fashion. If somebody had walked down Main Street dressed the way models dress in magazines, everyone would have stared. People who were too slickly turned out were almost objects of suspicion, and wearing effete extras like hats or gloves (except in awful weather) was considered eccentric. I wondered what the kids at the high school were going to make of Wyndy.

Chapter Two

When we got back to our house, we all helped carry the luggage inside. "Wyndy's arranged to have the rest of it sent by ship," I said to Dad.

Dad looked a little taken aback, but only said, "Very sensible."

"Not the car, though," Wyndy put in. "One of the company engineers is driving it down for me from New York. It should get in some time this evening. I wanted to drive it down myself but Sally wouldn't buy the idea."

"Do you have an American driver's license?" Mom asked.

"I've got an international license. That will do over here."

I could see Mom's pulse already starting to race with terror at the mere idea of Wyndy driving a car.

We stacked the beautiful suitcases at the door to his room. Dad gazed in at the ruffled curtains, the pink bedspread and the lacy pillow and said, "You'll be wanting to make some changes in your room, I expect. I believe we have some other curtains and bedspreads up in the attic."

I could sense that Wyndy was stifling the impulse to look curiously around him. Our house was rather a small one, which was fine because we were a small family, but maybe he was used to living in a gigantic, ancient palazzo or something. He could be wondering where the servants were and the long, tapestry-filled halls.

"Would you like some lunch?" Mom asked. "Or perhaps you'd like to lie down. I expect you're feeling the effects of jet lag."

"I had lunch on the plane, thank you," he said. "Maybe I'll lie down. I'm pretty much dead."

We left him to his nap and retreated to the kitchen together. Sitting around the table over our lunchtime ham sandwiches, we all looked at each other for a minute or two without saying a word. We were dying to talk about him, but it would have been awful if he had suddenly come into the kitchen and caught us at it.

Finally, Dad spoke. "He's a good-looking boy," he said slowly.

"Don't worry about it, Mom," I said. "He doesn't even see me. He looks right through me."

"I have to admit," she said, "that it has been a shock that he's a boy. I can't think how I could have gotten confused about that. It's all my fault. But since you bring it up, Jessica, I don't mind saying that he's far too old for you."

"Only a year or so," I said, suddenly on the defensive, "and I'm very mature for my age."

"Of course, dear, but Wyndy is *exceptionally*...that is, you are so fresh and unspoiled and he's . . . I don't know quite how to put this, but . . ."

"Oh, don't worry about it. He's not my type."

Mom looked more cheerful. "He *isn't* your type, that's true. All the boys you've had crushes on have been very sweet, now that I come to think of it."

Dad shot an anxious look at the kitchen door. "We don't want to make him feel unwelcome," Dad said. "What we've got to remember is that however self-sufficient he might look, he seems to have had a rough time and we ought to go out of our way to make him feel at home."

"Of course," said Mom promptly.

"Naturally," I said.

Wyndy didn't appear again for the rest of the afternoon. Mom debated with herself about whether to call him to dinner, but finally hearing sounds of movement inside his room, she did knock on his door. "Dinnertime, Wyndy," she called.

He came out right away. I almost suspected that he hadn't been napping at all but had just wanted to get away from us for a while.

"I hope you like fried chicken," said Mom as we all sat down.

"Love it," he said warmly. "Reminds me of my grandmother's. Makes me feel right at home."

Lots of people pick up fried chicken and eat it with their fingers, but I could have foretold that Wyndy wasn't going to be one of those. Instead, he began deftly cutting the meat off the bones. But unlike normal people who only turn their forks over when they're cutting meat, then quickly flip the fork right side up and switch it to their right hand for eating, he kept his fork turned over and in his left hand not just for cutting but also for spearing the chicken and even for eating his mashed potatoes. I had never seen anyone convey food to their mouth on the back of their fork before and I couldn't take my eyes off him. I had to admit his method was faster, not having to stop and switch the fork to the right hand every second or so, but it looked very strange. I was agog to find out what he would do with the peas. Would he flatten them on the back of the fork with his knife? Would he cement them on the back of the fork with a bit of mashed potatoes? I never did find out. It turned out when the peas were passed that he didn't care for them. I later found out that Wyndy's method of eating was standard enough in Europe, but at first glance it seemed strange enough to me to be Martian.

"Your mother told us about the attempt to kidnap you," Dad said, reaching for a biscuit. "That must have been pretty scary."

"Terrifying," said Wyndy, cheerfully buttering one for himself. "I was a wreck for weeks afterward. Just the sound of a creaking stair would set me off screaming."

"That's hard to believe," said Dad, looking amused. "But don't talk about it if you'd rather not."

"Oh, it doesn't bother me to talk about it, but the truth is it was over so fast I didn't even know what happened. I heard a pistol shot and when I looked up there was Ferreti, looking white as a sheet and running a red light. It was all over in a minute. I didn't see a thing." He polished off the last bit of his biscuit and reached for another.

"Did the police ever find the people who did it?" asked Mom.

"Not a hope," said Wyndy, "but then the police..." He dismissed Rome's finest with an eloquent wave of the hand.

"You aren't suggesting the police were paid off?" asked Mom.

"Hadn't thought of that," said Wyndy. "Could be. But no, probably not. We just didn't expect the police to get anywhere."

"The American police are very efficient," I put in.

He looked at me indulgently. "Better to count on people that you know," he said. "I knew we could count on Ferreti, our chauffeur, for example. He's worked for us for years and his sister Consuela works for us and so does his cousin Vittorio. Ferreti's got very quick reflexes. If it hadn't been for him, they'd have probably ended up finding my cold body in the trunk of a car somewhere." He calmly cut and speared another bit of chicken. "As for the police," he went on, "what's it to them? None of their business."

I couldn't understand him. If law and order weren't the business of the police, whose business were they? I didn't say anything, though. I knew I wouldn't change his weird point of view just by arguing with him, and besides, Mom and Dad were counting on me to make myself agreeable.

"The worst of it was," Wyndy went on, "that Sally insisted on hiring three bodyguards after that. Can you imagine going to the men's room with three bodyguards? Going out to buy a tube of toothpaste with three bodyguards? Going out with a girl with three bodyguards?'' He blanched a little at the memory. ''Couldn't stand it anymore. And it's not as if the bodyguards are any guarantee. Good Lord, the streets of Rome are practically choked with corpses of bodyguards that didn't cut it. I mean, if your number is up, it's up. Bodyguards aren't going to make any difference. But no use telling Sally that.''

I noticed he had changed out of the casual linen suit he had worn on the plane and was wearing, for a simple supper with the family, pleated linen slacks in a pale peach color and a thin, silk-weave shirt, a symphony of muted peach and lavender checks that had been left open to the fourth button. This outfit perfectly set off his dark good looks and called all the more attention to his face, with its high cheekbones and the dark brooding look his black-fringed eyes took on when he was trying to decide whether to have another biscuit or move on to dessert. I thought of all the clothes in those suitcases of his and in the luggage coming by boat, and wondered what it was going to be like to leave for school every morning with a boy who had more different things to wear than I did.

After careful reflection, he opted to skip the biscuit and begin at once on the chocolate cake, which Mom was serving up from the sideboard. ''Wonderful meal,'' he said. ''I'll have to go back and give my compliments to the cook.''

''But *I'm* the cook,'' said Mom.

He recovered quickly. ''A first-class one, too,'' he said. ''Terrific biscuits.''

Mom and Dad seemed to be warming to Wyndy, a development I had mixed feelings about. I supposed it wasn't surprising. I could see that he had a certain breezy charm. It just wasn't the kind of charm I went for. He was too smooth and self-confident by half.

''I suppose you must be wondering what courses you'll need to register for at school,'' said Dad.

From the startled look on Wyndy's face, I could see that was the last thing he was wondering about.

''Jessica can give you a rough idea of that,'' Dad said, ''and when you go in to school on Monday, you can go straight to

Myra Fenwick's office and she'll take care of getting you registered. She's one of the guidance counselors there. I gave her a call yesterday and told her you'd be coming in." Dad gave me a meaningful look. He evidently didn't think I was putting myself out enough to be helpful and friendly to Wyndy.

I chimed in obediently, "Do you think you'll want to take the regular college track courses? Or the accelerated program?"

"Which are you taking?"

"The accelerated," I said. "It looks better on your records. You've got to have a B average, though."

"No problem."

"Well, in the junior year, you've got to take English, American History, Algebra II, Chemistry, and a foreign language."

"Italian?" he asked, raising an eyebrow.

"No, they just offer French, Spanish, and Latin."

"Latin, then," he said, making a gesture with his fork. "Piece of cake. I've already had years of it." He paused a moment. "Maybe they'll exempt me from it. That way I could free up another hour for something more fun. You don't happen to know if they have fencing, do you?"

"I don't think they offer fencing," I said weakly.

His eyes took on that telltale triangular look. He was laughing at me. "You don't have to look at me that way," he said. "If I mess up everything, by the time anybody notices, I'll be moving on."

I brightened. "That's true." I would have to keep reminding myself that he wouldn't be with us forever.

We had no sooner finished dinner than I spotted Wyndy's new car being driven up in front of the house. I recognized it at once because it was quite different from the usual sort of car. I had seen people driving around in their father's little Corvettes or in Trans Ams or things like that, but this was in a different class—larger and longer with fat exhaust pipes, a front end that seemed to sneer at pedestrians, and an impossibly long expanse of glistening yellow finish.

Wyndy spotted it driving up, too, and went out the front door at once to meet the man who was getting out of it. I trailed behind him, drawn in spite of myself to its gleaming beauty.

"Thank you," Wyndy was saying to the man as he shook hands with him.

The man smiled. "Glad to help out, Mr. Sarto."

"You'll have to let me give you a lift to the car rental agency."

"You don't have to do that. Gino there, followed me down. I'm going to ride on with him."

I noticed then that a modest gray sedan had pulled up behind the sports car. A small, dark man with a moustache got out and was duly introduced to Wyndy and formally thanked.

"She's a beauty," said the car's driver, giving it a last affectionate glance. "We're still breaking her in, so I took it easy coming down."

Wyndy again thanked the men for their trouble, and as they drove off in the gray sedan, he sketched a majestic gesture of farewell in the air.

The big yellow car was remarkably clean for having driven such a long way south. Not a speck of grime marred its gleaming surface. Wyndy caressed it delicately with his fingertips. "Beautiful," he said with a look of pure pleasure. He caught my glance. "Gorgeous, huh?" he said.

"What is it called?"

"It's the Sarto Hirondelle 500."

"Very pretty."

His eyes laughed at me. Doubtless he had figured out that my relationship with cars was strictly of the it-gets-me-there-and-takes-me-back variety. I just wasn't very interested in cars. I hadn't even started to learn to drive yet, though in a few months I would be old enough to get a license.

His dark eyes fixed on my face. "Are you really disappointed I turned out not to be a girl?" he asked suddenly.

"It was a blow. But I can see you can't help it."

"Thank you," he said wryly. "What's the matter? Don't you like boys?"

"Of course I like boys. Why, some of my best friends are boys. It's just that I had been counting on a girl, that's all."

He ran his fingers absently over the car's gleaming surface. "Do you think your parents mind?"

I knew that in a way they did, but it wouldn't have been nice to say so. "Oh, no," I said. "It's just me. I guess I was disappointed because my best friend is going away to school, and I was . . . well, actually, it's a little difficult to explain," I said, letting my answer trail off. When I thought about how Audrey was probably unpacking her things at Chowan Hall right then, I felt pretty desolate. Not only was I all alone, I had this stranger living in my house. Someone who was more than strange, actually, more like an alien, a weird person who even ate funny.

"Want to go for a spin in the Hirondelle?"

I looked at the car's fat exhaust pipes and suppressed a shudder. I had no interest at all in getting into a car that could go at half the speed of light. The thing didn't even have a top. What if it rolled over?

"No, thank you."

He shrugged. "Suit yourself." He stepped into the car and took off down the street with a roar. After he'd disappeared from sight, I went back into the house.

"Wyndy's driven off in that new sports car they brought him," I told Mom. She was standing at the sink washing up. Dad was sitting at the kitchen table reading the paper.

"Oh, goodness," Mom said, distractedly. "So soon? I hope he has car insurance. Oh, surely . . . Did it look to you as if he knew how to drive the thing, Jess? Did he seem to be speeding? Oh, dear, I *wish* he didn't have a car. It's just one more thing to worry about."

"He seemed to know what he was doing. Maybe I'll go write a letter to Audrey."

"Don't go yet," said Mom. "We've got to decide what to do about church tomorrow. Of course, he would normally go with us, but maybe he's Catholic."

"Is Sally Catholic?"

"You mean, Mrs. Sarto, dear," Mom corrected me. "No, Sally's family was Presbyterian. But surely Giovanni . . . I think . . . Yes, Wyndy must be Catholic."

She reached for the phone book and turned to the yellow pages. "That's what I was afraid of. The masses at Immaculate Conception are at eight and ten-thirty. That is awkward. Our service doesn't start till eleven."

"Aren't you forgetting, Susan?" said Dad, lowering his newspaper. "The boy has his own car."

Mom's brow cleared. "Oh, yes, of course. But he won't know the way, and it seems inhospitable to send him to church by himself. Don't we know anybody he could go with? What about the O'Reillys? They're Catholic. I think I'll just give Margaret O'Reilly a call and explain the situation to her."

Thinking of the O'Reillys' five children and their tendency to get their sticky lollipops on other people's clothes, I decided to do Wyndy a favor. "I think you'd better wait, Mom, until you find out whether he wants to go with the O'Reillys," I said.

"Jess is right," said Dad. "We don't want to come across as overbearing. One or two things he said at dinner give me the idea Wyndy's parents have given him a very loose rein. We'd better move carefully at first if we don't want to risk alienating him."

When Wyndy returned from his trial run in the car, he invited us all to come out and admire it.

"Goodness," said Mom faintly. "I believe those hubcaps are exactly the sort that are always getting stolen at the shopping center. Perhaps you'd better not park it at the shopping center, Wyndy."

Only a momentary wave of disgust over his face indicated that Wyndy did not consider Mom's comment a fitting tribute to the Hirondelle. As usual, however, he bounced back quickly. "Want to go for a spin, Mr. MacAlister, Mrs. MacAlister?" he asked.

There were only two bucket seats in the car. "You go, Richard," said Mom, looking at the car with distrust. Soon Dad and Wyndy were roaring off together. A few minutes later they roared back, coming from the direction of Baker Street. Dad got out of the car with a strange glow in his eyes. "It certainly is a magnificent car," he said.

As we all walked back to the house, I heard Mom say, "Did you ask him about church?"

"It completely slipped my mind," said Dad. "Wyndy," he called, "would you like to go to church tomorrow with some friends of ours, the O'Reillys? You could go with us, of course, but we had the idea you might be Catholic."

Wyndy paused a second to wait for Mom and Dad to catch up with him. "I think I'll just sleep in tomorrow morning," he said.

"Of course, you don't have to go with the O'Reillys," Mom put in. "Immaculate Conception isn't really so difficult to find. You could just as easily go by yourself."

"I *always* sleep in on Sunday," said Wyndy.

"But isn't your father a Catholic?" asked Mom, unable to grapple at once with open insubordination from a guest in her home.

"Nope," said Wyndy firmly. "Pagan."

Mom and Dad immediately dropped the subject, and one thing began to be clear to me. Wyndy Sarto was going to get away with murder. I could imagine how the roof would have shook if I had announced that *I* always slept in on Sunday.

The next morning, my temper was not improved when I limped into the living room in some uncomfortable shoes I had gotten on sale only to see Wyndy coming out of his room with a leisurely yawn. He was barefoot and wearing a black silk robe embroidered with blue and gold threads. He saw that we were getting ready to leave and said, "Good morning. Don't let me hold you up, Mrs. MacAlister. I eat a very light breakfast. Just a croissant and maybe some cheese. I can manage it myself." He gave Mom an ingratiating smile.

Mom's brow wrinkled. "I'm afraid I don't have any croissants, Wyndy," she said. "There are some rolls on top of the refrigerator."

"Come on, Susan," said Dad. "He'll be okay. We're going to be late."

"Yes, don't worry about me," Wyndy said. "I'll manage."

When we got to church, I discovered I had suddenly become very popular. As we were going in Marian Beasley grabbed the chance to slide up to me. Marian is a world-class gossip. It is a point of pride with her to be first with the news. "Who belongs to that very fancy sports car in front of your house, Jessica?'' she asked. ''Have you got company?''

''Not exactly company,'' I answered cautiously. ''The son of a friend of Mom's is going to live with us for a while. Maybe not long,'' I added hopefully.

Marian's eyes opened wide. ''How old is he?'' she asked. ''What does he look like?''

''I think he's about seventeen and I guess he looks okay if you like the type.''

''I think I will,'' said Marian, licking her lips. ''What type is he?''

I thought about it a minute. ''Tall, dark and handsome,'' I said succinctly.

After the service, Karen Harper caught me on the way out of the building. ''Who's your company, Jessie? Tony told me there was a Hirondelle 500 parked outside your house. I told him I bet it belonged to that aunt of yours who's a lawyer. Right?''

''No,'' I said. ''It belongs to a good-looking boy who has come to live with us.''

She chuckled appreciatively. ''No, who does it really belong to?''

''*That's* who it really belongs to.''

Behind me I could hear Mom talking to the Johnsons. ''Son of a very dear old friend of mine,'' she was murmuring. ''We're putting him up in our spare room.''

It was obvious that the yellow car had caused quite a stir among those who had driven up Oak Street on their way to church.

''You have all the luck!'' cried Karen. ''What's he like?''

''He just got in yesterday. I've only just met him.''

''Is he shy?''

''Not exactly.''

''Just sort of shy?''

''Not really. You'll see him at school tomorrow and you can make up your own mind.''

She gnawed on a fingernail. "I won't be able to find *any-body* in all that confusion," she said. "I hope I don't get lost. The place is so big I'm not going to know which way to go!"

"We'll be all right," I said.

She sighed. "I wish I could be calm like you. I guess you and Audrey are really looking forward to it, huh?"

"You didn't hear? Audrey's going away to boarding school this year. To Chowan Hall. Her parents drove her over there yesterday. She was awfully excited about it."

"No!"

I quickly blinked tears away. "Yup. Well, I guess I'll see you tomorrow." I fled before I cracked up completely.

When we finally got to the car, Mom slid in the front seat and said, "Whew! I think half the town must have seen Wyndy's car."

"What did you tell people about him?" I asked.

"I just said he was the son of an old friend of mine," said Mom. "I don't see any reason to go into all that stuff about the kidnapping attempt or Sally's mountain climbing."

"Or Giovanni's sanitarium," Dad put in.

"Just so," said Mom. "It all sounds so lurid. We don't want people to get a lot of preconceived ideas about Wyndy. We want them to see him as just another ordinary boy, don't you think, Richard?"

"Oh, absolutely," said Dad. After a thoughtful moment he added, "Too bad about that car."

I could see what he meant. The Hirondelle was bound to detract somewhat from the impression that Wyndy was just an average kid.

When we got home, the long yellow hood of the Hirondelle was up and Wyndy appeared to be pointing out certain interesting aspects of the engine to Tony Harper, Karen's older brother. The two boys straightened up as we drove into the driveway, and when we got out of our car, Tony smiled at us. "Some car, huh?" he said. I reflected that this was three more words than Tony had spoken to me in the entire previous year.

He was a big, heavily muscled guy, and since I read the local paper I knew that he was a valued tackle on the Senior High football team. Also, Karen had once told me proudly that Tony was a big deal at Senior High, a bit of news that hadn't made me feel optimistic about the social atmosphere there. My personal knowledge of him was very limited, however, because whenever Karen and I happened to be in their house working on homework or something, he immediately disappeared out the back door and was soon roaring down Oak Street polluting the atmosphere with smoke from his old car.

It was pretty clear that even the Hirondelle wouldn't hold him in our yard long enough to chat. "See you," he said, and at once began jogging back to his own house.

"Tony and I thought we'd play a couple of sets of tennis after lunch," Wyndy said. "If that's okay with you, that is."

"That's just fine," said Mom. "There's only one thing. Uh, Wyndy, I wouldn't let Tony drive your car. Anybody will tell you he's a perfect menace on the road."

"No danger," said Wyndy, smiling. "I'm not going to let anybody wreck the Hirondelle but me."

Mom winced. He hadn't chosen the most reassuring way of framing his reply.

"That car is making you famous," Dad said, opening the door for us to go inside. "People at church kept asking about it."

"You don't see many Hirondelles around," Wyndy admitted, looking smug.

I helped Mom set the table while Dad and Wyndy started a game of chess. That was precisely the sort of sexist arrangement that Audrey was always foaming at the mouth about, and I could see why. I didn't mind when Dad sat down while Mom and I set the table because I knew that he did all kinds of unpleasant things that we didn't have to do. He was the one who had climbed under the house, for example, when the pipes froze last winter and had to be defrosted with a blowtorch. And he was the one who always knocked down the wasps' nests in summer. But Wyndy had positively no excuse for sitting there doing nothing.

I could see it was sort of an awkward situation. He was a guest in a way, but in a way he wasn't. Maybe Mom didn't like to ask him to help out. It did seem to me he should have offered, though.

When Mom and I put on the baked ham, green beans and sweet potatoes, Wyndy and Dad gravitated toward the table, laughing. I tried to tell myself it was nice they were getting along so well.

"Oh, I told Tony I'd give him a ride to school tomorrow," Wyndy said, pulling out a chair.

"Are you sure you don't want to take the bus?" Mom said. "Jessica always takes the bus. It stops right in front of the house."

Of course, from Mom's point of view the school bus was ideal. It never went over forty-five miles an hour, the riders were, at least theoretically, under adult supervision, and you knew that if they got on the school bus they were truly going to school and not to the pool hall. Since I understood how her mind worked, I had no difficulty understanding why she had asked if he wouldn't prefer the bus. But Dad and Wyndy looked at her as if she were out of her mind.

"Don't be absurd, Susan," Dad said sharply. "Of course, he'll drive his car."

"I hope his hubcaps don't get stolen," said Mom, firing a feeble parting shot.

Wyndy looked at me from under his dark lashes. "I forgot Jessica would need a ride tomorrow," he said. "I guess I shouldn't have offered that ride to Tony. Would you like to straddle the gearshift, Jessica? I can squeeze in one more."

"No, thank you," I said, unfolding the napkin in my lap. "I love taking the school bus." I was a little afraid that Dad might view this comment as sarcastic and come down on me later for being rude, so I added quickly, "It's a real slice of Americana, the school bus. A tradition. And you get to visit with your friends before school. When there's a fight on the bus, it can even be exciting."

"What's this about fights on the bus, Jessica?" asked Mom with an anxious look.

"Arguments, I mean, Mom. Not knives or anything."

"Too bad," said Wyndy, serving himself a slice of ham. "It sounded interesting there for a minute."

After lunch, Wyndy went to his room and changed into a tennis outfit of blinding whiteness, its cotton sweater top adorned only by a thin band of blue along the lower edge. He drove off to get Tony and I helped Mom clean up, then Mom and I washed and folded some clothes. When we were finished, I realized I felt a little flat. Wyndy was annoying, but watching him continue on his exasperating way seemed to give focus to the day. Without him around to be annoyed at, the afternoon seemed to stretch long and empty before me.

I went out back and hung over the white fence that separated our yard from the Fieldses' yard.

"Hi, Peter!" I called.

The love of my life, Peter Fields, looked around, saw me, and sneezed.

"God bless you," I said. "Are you getting set up to take pictures?"

He looked pained. "Photos, Jess. Or 'shots.' *Not* 'pictures.'"

"I'm sorry," I said humbly.

Peter sneezed twice in succession and wiped his nose with a large white handkerchief.

"You should take your allergy medicine," I said. "This is the ragweed season."

"I forgot," he said. "And now I'm too busy getting set up."

I could see that the Fieldses' grape arbor was elaborately draped with lengths of chiffon material. Crumpled tinfoil had been wedged in at intervals between the entwined vine stems, and the presence of some tall lights and a few white, umbrella-shaped reflectors showed that Peter had readied his backyard for yet another photo session. I would have thought that Peter would get tired of photographing pretty girls, or alternatively that they would get tired of being photographed. But so far there had been no sign of either happening.

"You should go in and get a pill now," I said.

"I can't. Brandi could get here any minute and I told her to come right on back to the grape arbor."

I climbed over the fence. "I'll go get it for you," I said.

"Thanks, Jess," he said gratefully.

I went on in the back door of the Fieldses' house and told Mrs. F. I would take Peter's antihistamine to him. A few minutes later I was holding out some little red pills to him. Brandi had arrived while I was in the house and was now arranging herself in front of the grape arbor, stretching out her long legs and pursing her lips in a winsome pout. Peter bolted the pill, swallowed some water in a couple of convulsive mouthfuls, then went back to adjusting his lights.

"This one shines down on your hair," he explained to Brandi, "and makes it shine. And this one diffuses the light on your face so I don't get any unbecoming shadows."

Brandi, who was wearing her majorette costume for the photo session, looked suitably impressed. She patted her fluffy blond hair, which curled softly around her earlobes. I noticed that she had a rather weak chin.

I stood at Peter's elbow, pondering on his taste for blondes. Perhaps what my hair needed was a good bleach job. On the other hand, the possibility that Peter might fall for me if I went blond had to be balanced against the certainty that my father would kill me if I did.

Peter was intent on his work. Beads of sweat were beginning to form on his upper lip as he arranged lights, rearranged tinfoil, and asked Brandi to raise her chin. He was a boy of medium height, a bit on the bony side, with untidy brown hair and an angelic smile. I had always felt that he was a real artist. He snapped a few shots, asked Brandi to lick her lips and shot a few more.

The only problem with Peter was that sometimes the details escaped him. I tapped him gently on the shoulder.

"Don't bother me now, Jess," he said. "Can't you see I'm busy?"

I pointed silently to the film rewind knob on the camera. He watched the knob for a second, then gulped. "Just a minute, Brandi," he said. He turned his back on her and, taking a roll of film from his pants pocket quickly loaded the camera. I looked benignly over his shoulder to make sure the film was properly engaged in the sprockets before he slammed the back of the camera closed.

I thought he was smart not to tell Brandi that the last ten shots had been blanks. I flashed her a smile then went over and perched on the fence.

"Aren't you ready yet, Peter?" Brandi asked. "I'm getting a crick in my neck."

"Just a minute," he said. "Okay, that's terrific. Stay just the way you are. You look beautiful."

After watching them for quite a while, I finally went back into the house. It was nice to know that there was at least one person who hadn't noticed the yellow sports car in front of our house. Peter was totally absorbed in his art.

I decided to make good use of my free time by washing my hair. Monday was the first day of school and I wanted to look spiffy. After my hair was dry I would go back and check on Peter to see if he needed any help cleaning up all that aluminum foil and chiffon.

I had no sooner got in the house than Wyndy came in the front door. From the cheerful way he was swinging his racket, I deduced he had won. Dad looked up from his book. "How'd it go?" he asked.

"Tony's backhand is a joke," he said. He grinned suddenly. "In fact, his whole game's a joke."

I closed the door to my room and pulled my old terry-cloth bathrobe out of my closet. It would be nice, I thought, if Wyndy were to run into somebody he didn't feel superior to. I hoped I'd be there to see it when it happened.

When I came out of my room with my bathrobe over my arm, I could hear the sound of the shower going full force in the bathroom.

"Wyndy's taking a shower," Dad explained, not looking up from his book.

"I was going to wash my hair," I said.

"You don't have to stand there looking outraged," Dad said. "How long can it take him to get a shower?"

Quite a while, as it turned out. After the shower had run long enough to convince me that he had used up all the hot water, I heard the telltale high-pitched whine of a hair dryer inside the bathroom. Still he didn't come out.

"Maybe he's giving himself a facial," I told Dad.

"Good grief, Jessica," Dad said, "anybody would think you were suffering a terrible hardship to have to share a bathroom. Why, when I was growing up, there were five of us kids and the whole family used one bathroom."

"You must have been very dirty kids."

"I don't say it wasn't inconvenient. But we managed all right. All that's needed is a little give and take."

I could tell who was going to do all the taking in the present setup. Wyndy was showing all the signs of being one of those people who are never happier than when their pores are soaking up steam. I would probably end up having to go down to Karen's house to take my baths for the duration of his stay.

Finally, he emerged from the bathroom, his black-silk-clothed figure barely visible in the vast cloud of steam that engulfed him as he came out the door. After he had disappeared into his room, I stepped in and turned on the hot water faucet. Just as I had suspected—stone cold.

"The water's cold," I reported back to Dad in the living room.

"It will warm up again," he said.

It was true that in another hour or so it would be warm again, of course, but what if Wyndy decided to take the second installment of his bath? I knew that lots of people took a regular bath at night even if they had had a shower earlier in the day. The thought of going to my first day at Senior High with stringy hair made me feel weak at the knees.

I sat down near Dad in the living room and read the Sunday comics, waiting for the water to warm up and trying hard to be philosophical about the recent reverses in my life. To think that only a week ago I was an only child with a bathroom all to herself. I had also had a close friend that I could share my troubles with and another week of summer vacation left. And now? Now I felt like one of those movie heroes who finds himself out in the middle of the jungle with nothing but a few rags and a hunting knife.

The water was taking forever to warm up. I remembered that I had planned to check on Peter, so I went out back and leaned over the fence again. Peter was sprawled in a lawn chair in the midst of all the crumpled aluminum foil, wiping his nose. There was no sign of Brandi.

"Finished for the day?" I asked him.

"Yup. Just now. I think I got some decent shots. Now all I've got to do is clean this mess up."

"Want some help?"

"That would be great," he said, sneezing into his handkerchief.

"It won't take us long," I said.

He dragged himself out of the chair. "It's this hay fever," he said. "I can hardly breathe."

"Tsk, tsk," I said sympathetically. "Well, you start over there and I'll start here, and we'll be finished in no time."

"I don't know what I'd do without you, Jess," he said.

I smiled at him. Peter was not at his best during the allergy season, but even when his nose was pink I liked to look at him. There was a lovely curve to his lips and chin and a confiding expression in his brown eyes. In spite of his long, lanky legs and his tendency to trip on his untied shoelaces, there was something very sweet about him.

"How did the pictures, I mean, the shots of Susannah come out?" I asked. "The ones you took last week."

His eyes lit up. "The color ones were terrific. Want to take a look at them? I don't know what went wrong with the black-and-white roll. I must have done something wrong in the developing room."

I found that all too easy to believe. Peter did not have the temperament for careful chemical procedures. "You didn't forget and turn on the light, did you?"

"No," he said. "I think it was something to do with the fixing solution." He shot a speculative look at me. "You're good at that kind of thing, Jess. How would you like to learn to develop?"

We had done some photo development in general science and from what I remembered it didn't seem that difficult. If I did

Peter's developing he would really be dependent on me then. Maybe he would keep coming over to ask when his prints would be ready. Maybe we would spend cozy moments discussing developing techniques.

"I'd let you use all my equipment and everything," he said, "and all you'd have to do would be to develop a couple of rolls a week for me. It's really kind of fun."

"I don't think I'd better," I said. "We've got a houseguest staying with us and the bathroom is pretty well tied up as it is."

"But maybe after the houseguest leaves?"

"That could be a long time from now," I said. "It's all kind of up in the air. I'd better not make any plans."

He smoothed out a few sheets of aluminum foil and clipped them together with a clothespin to store for reuse. "Think about it, anyway. Who is this houseguest?"

"The son of a friend of my mother's. He's going to be a junior this year."

Peter's mind seemed to have already wandered from the matter of the houseguest. "I wonder if I should have tried some shots from a ladder?" he said. "I need to try some new camera angles. I feel as though I'm getting stale."

After Peter and I had everything tidied up and stored away, I climbed back over the fence and headed home. I saw that Wyndy had come out back and was sitting on the low wall of our terrace, one leg propped up and one bare leg dangling. He was wearing the black silk bathrobe. Sitting next to Wyndy was Mrs. Henniker's black cat, having a nice stretch in the sunshine. Wyndy seemed to have been trimming his nails. He snapped the nail clippers shut as I came up to him.

"Who lives on the other side of the fence?" he asked.

"The Fieldses."

"And you've been visiting?"

"I sometimes help Peter Fields with his photography," I said.

"Do I get to meet this Fields guy?"

"I suppose you might," I said. "We'll all be going to the same school."

Wyndy gave me a knowing look. "You like him, huh?"

I was torn between the desire to keep my personal life private and the desire to show Wyndy that the sort of boy I admired was quite different from him. My baser instincts won out. "Yes," I said. "Peter's a sensitive, artistic person. I like that sort of boy."

"You two go together?"

"We have a platonic relationship."

He shrugged. "Well, if you get tired of platonic I might be able to help you out there."

Iciness stole into my voice. "I don't see what you mean."

"I could give you the male point of view. Maybe you're going at it all wrong."

"Thank you," I said, "but I'm very happy with the way things are."

He tucked the fingernail clippers into the pocket of his robe. "Just keep it in mind."

Chapter Three

Karen was already at the bus stop in front of our house. It was easy to see that she, like me, had just washed her hair because a few unruly wisps were being lifted by the morning breeze. She had obviously made a real effort to look good for the first day of school. Her shirt was freshly pressed and her skirt was brand-new. It was hard for me to put my finger on why, after all that, she didn't look perfectly turned out the way Wyndy had when he had left the house earlier in the morning. Money might be part of the answer. Wyndy's clothes must have cost a fortune. But as I inspected Karen, looking slapdash in spite of her best efforts, I had to admit that maybe there was an art to wearing clothes. I uneasily gave another tuck to my shirttail and twisted around to make sure no threads were trailing my skirt's hem.

"I'm nervous," Karen said, gnawing at her thumbnail. "Aren't you even a little bit nervous, Jessica?"

I refused to admit it. "I expect it'll be a lot of fun going to Senior High," I said.

"Wyndham gave Tony a ride to school today," she said. "I guess you must know that. I was kind of surprised he was giving Tony a ride instead of you. It was a good thing for me, though. I thought I'd end up waiting all alone for the bus this morning."

"Wyndy and I each go our own ways," I said. "He just happens to live in the same house."

"That's funny," she said. "Don't you like him?"

I was tempted to express myself freely on this subject but I caught myself just in time. Mom and Dad would not like it if I went around telling everybody that I didn't like Wyndy. More important, Wyndy would not like it, and it would be easy for him to retaliate. He could tell all the junior boys that I was horrible. He could move into the bathroom permanently.

"I like him okay," I said. "Of course, he just got here. We hardly know each other."

"Somehow I get the idea you don't like him."

"Oh, no," I said, smiling falsely. "I don't know how you got that idea."

When the bus arrived, it turned out we had a new bus driver, a middle-aged lady who was apparently used to a lot of peace and quiet. For one nasty moment on the way to school it looked as if she might fall apart, but somehow she managed and we got there all right. She pulled up in the circular drive in front of Senior High, opened the bus door, and we began pouring out.

Things seemed awfully confusing at first. There were people everywhere and a lot of noise. "I wonder where we go," said Karen, looking around her. Suddenly I heard a loud chanting coming from high up. I looked up and saw a bunch of kids were on the roof of the building making a terrific racket.

I looked them over. Taken individually, they weren't very impressive looking. Most of them were wearing shorts and old T-shirts with Senior painted on them, although I did see one dissenting T-shirt with a red maple leaf that said Canada. One of the guys dancing to the blaring jam box was wearing swim trunks with a pink cummerbund and a black dinner jacket, the final touch to his outfit being given by a Burger King paper crown.

"They don't seem to have a dress code here," I observed to Karen.

"Look at *those*," she said, pointing to a smaller group over near a ventilation chimney. I could see they were more sinister than the kids in the larger group. For one thing, they were smiling nastily and for another they were carrying a long sign that said Sophbusters.

"I don't like their looks much," I agreed, "but I don't see how they can give us much trouble."

My calm did not last, however. My eye drifted over past the ventilation chimney and I spotted a familiar, well-dressed figure leaning lazily against some clerestory windows. "It's Wyndy!" I yelped. "What's he doing there? He's not a senior."

Karen followed my gaze. "Oh, they made him an honorary senior. Tony told me about it last night. They wanted to use the Hirondelle in their parade, that's why."

"Parade?"

"Sure," said Karen. "You know, the parade they do down Pine Street on the way to the school. The seniors do it every year. It's a tradition. That's why Tony and Wyndham had to leave so early this morning."

"I don't know what we're doing wasting time looking at this silly demonstration," I said. "We ought to be figuring out where to go next. The bell will be ringing any minute." I pulled out of my purse the course schedule that had been mailed to me weeks before. This was not easy as I kept getting jostled by people who were so busy looking at the roof that they didn't see me. Holding the course schedule in my hand, I headed purposefully toward the front door of the building. Karen trailed behind me.

"Naturally, they're excited about being seniors," she said wistfully. "Gee, I wish I were a senior—or even a junior."

I had heard that sophomores were the lowest of the low at Senior High. That was one of the things I had dreaded about the place. It didn't really hit me until I saw Wyndy up on the roof how much I disliked being the lowest of the low. Why, this was going to be like going to school with hundreds of Wyndys!

Hundreds of people acting condescending to me! Hundreds of people acting as if I were five years old! The idea was very unpleasant, in fact it was unbearable. I found myself thinking that it was time for a few changes at Senior High. Reforms were needed. I was going to have to give the matter some serious thought.

Most of the underclassmen were still outside the school building watching the show the seniors were putting on, so the halls were almost empty. "Who do you have for homeroom?" I asked Karen.

"Mrs. Grooms."

"Same as me. What we ought to do is find her class. That way we'll avoid the mad rush when the bell rings. It's room A-101. It ought to be in this building somewhere. Oh, look!" I glanced over the doorjamb of a room we were passing. "I think this is it." A-101 was stenciled in black paint over the door. We had found Grooms's class.

The eight o'clock bell went off like a bomb.

"We can go in now and get a good seat," I said.

Karen looked anxiously toward the front of the building. "I don't know. Maybe we should have waited and come in with everybody else."

"Oh, for heaven's sake, come on!" I said, pulling her into the room. "Do you want to get trampled in the stampede?"

As it turned out, though, there was no stampede. Karen and I had to sit in the room for several minutes before anybody else arrived. At last, Mac MacInroe stuck his head in the door. "Is this Grooms's class?" he asked. Mac was a big, amiable, teddy bear type with curly light-brown hair and a small gap between his two front teeth.

"I think so," I said.

"Whew," he said. "Found it at last." He heaved himself down beside me. "Say, Jess," he said, "Tony tells me you know that new guy, the one that's got the Hirondelle."

"Not really," I said. "He's just staying with my parents. He only got in on Saturday. His name is Wyndham Sarto, and he's the son of my mother's oldest friend."

"Sarto? Say, the Hirondelle's put out by Sarto. I wonder if there's any connection?"

I wasn't sure Wyndy wanted everybody at school to know that he was the Sarto of Sarto Motors so I didn't know what to say to that, but luckily at that point Mrs. Grooms came in. She was a plump woman with silvery hair, wearing a sleeveless flowered dress that was draped with six or eight ropes of colored beads. She smiled warmly at the three of us.

Our classmates began filing in, among them was Peter Fields, looking as if he weren't sure he had the right school, let alone the right room. I smiled at him. He smiled back, but sat down next to Nella Parvin, naturally, a blonde.

"Now, people," said Mrs. Grooms, when the classroom was almost full. "I want to welcome you all to Senior High. I hope you're going to have a rewarding year here. You'll come to homeroom every morning except for alternate Fridays when we have assemblies, and on those days you'll go directly to the auditorium." She put on her glasses and began reading from a thick stack of papers. "I have just a few announcements," she said.

These seemed to take most of the class. When the bell rang, we all went out into the hall. "What do you have next?" asked Karen, obviously unwilling to let go of me. I glanced at my schedule. "Biology, Mr. Doyle, C-107," I said.

"Golly, I'm so tired already and we've only just finished homeroom." Karen groaned. "How am I going to make it through the day? Where can C Building be?"

"Let's just ask somebody," I said. "Excuse me," I said to a passing boy. "Could you tell me...?" Suddenly I noticed he was wearing a circular bit of cardboard on his shirt with the legend Sophbuster on it and my voice trailed off.

Karen evidently hadn't noticed because she chimed in breathlessly, "Where is C Building?"

"Just take the elevator," said the boy cheerfully as he moved on.

"Oh, thanks," said Karen.

I glared at her.

"Didn't you hear him?" she said. "We just take the elevator!" She pointed to a hand-lettered sign ahead of us saying ELEVATOR.

"Karen," I said, "these are one-story buildings."

Her face crumpled. "Oh. That's right. I remember. Well, how are we going to find C Building then?"

"We'll look for it," I said. I followed a stream of students and we had the good luck to find ourselves going out of A Building onto a covered walkway. The building ahead of us was labeled with a hand-lettered sign saying B Building.

"We're getting warm," I said.

"How do we know we can trust this sign?" Karen asked.

"We don't. But it makes sense. The main building was A Building and this is the next one to it. Maybe the one just past this one will turn out to be C Building."

"We can check it by looking at the stenciled room numbers," she said, her eyes narrowing.

I only saw Wyndy once all morning. That was before lunch when I had just succeeded in finding my English class, Mrs. Grimsby, A-110. I was holding onto the doorknob to keep myself from being swept past the room by the surging mass of students in the hallway. I couldn't believe he had any idea where he was going, but he had the expression of a surfer riding the perfect wave. At first I couldn't understand it. Then I spotted the beautiful blonde who was talking to him. I only got a brief glimpse as they passed me, but I could see she was a natural platinum blonde with the sad, serene look of a Madonna in religious paintings. All became clear. Somebody was showing Wyndy his way to class; somebody who obviously knew all the ropes and then some.

"Hey, Jess," said Mac. "You got Grimsby this period, too? Hey, Jess, wake up! Is something wrong?"

"Nope," I answered curtly.

Just then, my attention was caught by a bulletin posted outside Mrs. Grimsby's door, announcing a statewide short story contest for teens being held by *Goblin Magazine*. A horror story. I had never written one before, but after my first day at Senior High I was really in the mood to produce a horror story.

Maybe I would enter. After all, I had won the ninth grade essay contest and this was a much more interesting theme than "The American Dream: Myth or Promise."

I jotted down the address of *Goblin Magazine* in my notebook. Then the bell rang with a deafening jangle and I had to go on into class.

I would have liked to give the contest some deeper thought, but Mrs. Grimsby was launching quickly into the background of *Beowulf* and I had to scramble quickly to get my notebook open and start taking notes.

When the bell rang marking the end of fourth period, Karen appeared at my side. "Now we've got to find the cafeteria," she said.

I gathered my books together and stood up. "It shouldn't be too hard. Everybody's going to be going in the same direction. All we do is follow the herd."

Karen shook her head. "No," she said. "Only sophomores go to the cafeteria. Everybody else gets in a car and goes someplace better."

I thought at first she was exaggerating. There had to be some juniors and seniors without wheels, I thought. But it didn't take me long to see that the mass exodus was leading outside the building to the parking lots. Only the sophomores seemed to be left behind. And I didn't know whether we could trust the hand-lettered sign that said Cafeteria—or not.

"Let's chance it," I said finally.

We were in luck. We had found one of the few honest hand-lettered signs in the building. We were soon walking into the cafeteria. As we pushed open the door, Karen said dramatically, "See! Just sophomores."

My heart sank as I looked around swiftly and saw so many of the old familiar faces from Johnson Junior High. There were some faces I didn't know, but it was pretty obvious they were from West Side Junior High. Karen had been right. There were only sophomores in the cafeteria. When Karen and I got through the line, we looked around for someone we knew. I finally spotted Marian's frizzy hair. Her body wave had obviously bombed. Now I was even more afraid that that was not what *my* hair needed. "Let's go sit with Marian and Holly," I said to Karen.

"Hey, there," said Marian as we pulled up chairs next to them. "I thought you'd be getting a ride out to lunch in that fantastic yellow car."

I was already regretting that we had decided to sit with Marian.

"Jessica and Wyndham go their separate ways," explained Karen.

"Really?" said Marian, her nose twitching slightly as she scented news. "Why is that?"

"No reason," I said. "After all, we hardly know each other. He only just flew in Saturday."

Marian was not discouraged by this. "You know him better than anybody else," she said. "You live in the same house."

"It doesn't follow," said Karen suddenly. "I've lived with Tony my whole life and we don't have much to do with each other at all. I'll bet he couldn't even pick me out of a lineup. I'll bet he couldn't identify my body, if he had to."

I noticed Karen's mind was taking on a rather morbid cast. Maybe it was the meat loaf.

"I'll tell you who he's in tight with," said Marian.

Karen blinked. "Who? Tony?"

"No, dummy. Jess's friend with the yellow sports car," Marian said. "Good old what's-his-name."

"Wyndham," I supplied. I realized that we were all leaning expectantly toward Marian, which was just what she loved. I forced myself to assume an appearance of unconcern.

Having paused enough for emphasis, Marian said, "Angela Nicholson."

"No!" said Holly.

"Who's Angela Nicholson?" I asked.

"She's a junior," supplied Karen. "Tony went out with her once or twice. The reason I heard about it was that Mom and Dad didn't like her."

"Really?" said Marian, her eyes lighting up.

I foresaw a great future for Marian as a reporter for the *National Enquirer*.

"Her family's got a lot of money," said Karen, "and I think Mom and Dad thought she was wild."

Marian looked around discontentedly. "All the sophomores are in here today," she said, "but tomorrow the crowd will be thinning out and the only people who'll be left will be the ones who can't get rides with upperclassmen; the losers; the meat loaf eaters."

"You know," I said, "these senior privileges seem un-American to me."

"But you can't stop the juniors and seniors from going out for lunch," said Karen. "That's not senior privileges. They've just got driver's licenses and we don't."

"I think some schools make everybody eat in the cafeteria," I said.

Karen looked at her meat loaf. "Oh, I wouldn't do that to anybody."

"Okay, maybe nothing can be done about the lunch problem," I conceded. "But all these other things—the senior privileges—that's just aggravation we don't need."

"It's traditional for seniors to have privileges," said Holly. "If they did away with senior privileges then we wouldn't get any privileges ourselves when we got to be seniors."

"Everybody ought to get privileges or nobody ought to get them," I said.

They looked at me as if I were nuts. I could see that a major job of reeducation was going to be needed before any changes could be made around here. You can't very well free the serfs if they don't even know they want to be free.

"What I think," said Marian, "is that we all ought to concentrate on getting rides out to lunch tomorrow. Karen, Tony has lots of room in that big old car of his. Now, do you think he'd like to have a few nice girls to keep him company?"

"Tony *has* a few nice girls to keep him company," said Karen plaintively, "and they aren't us."

"If Tony's out, then I guess we can't expect to snag a ride for four," said Marian. "I say it's every woman for herself tomorrow."

"I wonder if I could get to Burger King on a bicycle," said Karen.

When I got home after school, Wyndy was already home. Naturally, he got home first. The school bus only went forty-five miles per hour, and it stopped fifteen times to let people off. Also, it was not air-conditioned. I could feel a drop of sweat making its way down my forehead as I threw my half ton on the living-room floor and collapsed. Wyndy, already showered and changed into shorts, was lounging in the rocking chair, a cold drink in his hand.

He looked at me compassionately. "Why don't I give you a ride to school tomorrow, huh?"

"Oh, would you?" I said, throwing pride to the winds.

"Sure," he said.

"I'll be happy to straddle the gearshift."

"Won't have to. Tony's not going with me. He's got his own car. He just wanted to see the Hirondelle put through her paces." He paused. "Unless you need a ride to lunch, too. You'd have to straddle the gearshift at lunch."

"Wyndy, that is so nice of you! I would love a ride to lunch. I only ate one bite of that awful meat loaf and I still feel kind of sick."

"Meat loaf? What's that? Some regional dish?"

"You don't want to know about meat loaf."

"The reason you have to straddle the gearshift at lunch is because I'll be giving a ride to Angela."

"Oh. Doesn't Angela have her own car?"

"A little Trans Am," he said indulgently. "But she's riding with me and leaving her car at school." He smiled. "That's because we want to be together."

"I'm happy for you." If the two of them wanted to be together, I didn't see where I fitted in, stuck between them over the gearshift, but I thought it best not to point out this little difficulty to Wyndy. It was up to him to deal with Angela. All I cared about was not having to eat lunch in the cafeteria.

Chapter Four

The next morning I woke with the vague feeling that this day was going to be better than the day before. Then I remembered why. I wasn't going to have to eat in the school cafeteria. I jumped out of bed, slid quickly into jeans and a shirt and, looking in the mirror, ran a brush through my hair. My hair looked far from glamorous, but I knew it would look worse after I had ridden to school in an open car, so I began groping in my drawer for the cotton bandanna I had worn when I helped Mom paint the house trim. I fished it out triumphantly. It was a little wrinkled, but it would do. With the white design on the blue background, you hardly noticed the smear of white paint that had gotten on it. I stuffed it in my jeans pocket and dashed out to get some breakfast.

Wyndy was already in the kitchen, leisurely biting into one of the croissants Mom had bought for him. He never seemed to be in a hurry. It was one of the many annoying things about him. Mom was bending over a pot on the stove.

"Cocoa?" It didn't seem like cocoa weather. The sun was already beating hot outside the kitchen window.

She looked up at me. "Cappuccino," she said. "Hot milk and coffee mixed with a sprinkle of cocoa."

"Delicious," said Wyndy. "Try some."

"No, thank you," I said. I didn't see why Wyndy couldn't eat Rice Krispies like everybody else.

I shook my cereal in my bowl and tried to dwell on the advantages of having Wyndy around. He *was* going to give me a ride to school. The thing to do was to concentrate on that and not get annoyed about the small things.

Out the kitchen window I saw Karen getting on the school bus alone. I gulped a few mouthfuls of cereal. "Shouldn't we be going?" I said.

"No rush," said Wyndy. Mom poured the cappuccino into his cup and he began sipping it with the air of one for whom time has lost all meaning.

I finished my Rice Krispies. I gathered my books together. I looked uneasily out the window. I reshuffled my books. Finally, Wyndy took his last sip of coffee and announced he was ready to go.

As we got into the Hirondelle, I could see Mom's face peering anxiously out the kitchen window. I realized at once that Wyndy's plan was to make up on the road the time he had lost lingering over his cappuccino, but luckily for Mom's peace of mind, we didn't start to pick up speed until we turned the corner. Then we really took off.

It was an odd sensation to be sunk deep into the leather seat of the Hirondelle, feeling as if we were just barely clearing the pavement beneath us. I tried to tell myself that it was only because we were close to the ground that the pavement seemed to be whooshing by at such a ferocious rate. The car was so low that if we had hit a pedestrian (which at times seemed likely) we would have just about fractured his kneecaps. I stole a surreptitious look at the speedometer, then quickly closed my eyes.

Suddenly, I remembered my cotton bandanna and fished it out of my jeans pocket. Wyndy cast me a curious glance as I tied it over my windblown hair. I noted with envy that only a few locks of his hair had come disarranged and that they had fallen in a winning way over one eyebrow. My own hair, on the other hand, must be looking by now like a dish mop that had been pulled too late from the blades of the garbage disposal.

The car slowed. "I hear the cops have Sixteenth Street staked out," Wyndy explained. "You've got to be careful when you drive a car like this. I don't know—something about it makes the cops just love to pull you in."

If this ride was an example of his being really careful, I was glad I hadn't been in the car when he was being reckless. We turned onto Sixteenth Street and drove at a sedate pace past a waiting police car.

"I personally think it's good to obey the speed limit even if the police aren't watching you," I said primly. "It's the law, after all."

Wyndy just smiled indulgently at me and as soon as we lost sight of the police car he stepped hard on the gas. A few minutes later, we pulled into a space in the juniors' parking lot and I got out, my knees feeling weak.

Wyndy whipped a comb out of his pants pocket and looking in the rearview mirror subdued his fallen locks into their usual smoothness. Today he was wearing a lilac-colored T-shirt with three-quarter length sleeves and a short row of tiny buttons down the front. Naturally, none of the buttons were buttoned. "We'd better synchronize watches," he said as he got out. "We've only got forty minutes for lunch, so be at the car at noon on the dot. I don't like to have to rush over my food." He glanced at his wafer-thin gold watch. "I have seven fifty-seven and a half," he said.

After this warning, I knew better than to be late, so when noon came around I was at the car. Wyndy was, too. Only Angela was missing. Wyndy kept looking in the direction of the school building, his brows twisted into straight, annoyed lines. "I wonder what's holding her up?" he said. Cars whizzed past us in the parking lot. Everybody was dashing off like mad in order to get back by twelve-forty. Five minutes ticked away. He looked at his watch again. "I'm going to give her two minutes, and then we're leaving," he said.

Just then I spotted Angela's flaxen head bobbing along past the cars. She came up to us with a sweet smile, her hair in tight

French braids close to her head. "I hope I'm not too late," she whispered in her soft, breathy voice.

Wyndy flashed his white teeth. *"Cara mia,"* he said, "you are worth waiting for." He put his hand on my head. "This is Jessica," he said. "She's going to ride over the gearshift. She shouldn't be much in the way. She's small."

Swallowing my pride, I scrambled into the car, wedging myself between the two seats and scrunching my feet up close to me so Wyndy could change gears.

As we sped out of the parking lot, he looked over at Angela, blew an invisible kiss off his fingertips and said, *"Bella! Bellissima!"*

I cast him a surprised glance. What was it with all these tidbits of Italian all of a sudden? I had never heard him say anything in Italian before.

"I'm really sorry I was late," Angela said. "You don't think we'll have trouble getting back on time, do you?"

"Non importa," said Wyndy. "We'll make it up on the straightaway."

Angela smiled placidly. She was not pretty in the standard way, I noticed, but rather unusual looking, with heavy-lidded, almond-shaped eyes and high-arched eyebrows. She had pale skin and a small mouth with lips beautifully curved into a sad, sweet expression.

Then I screwed my eyes closed as Wyndy hit the highway and proceeded to make up the time we had lost by cutting in and out between other speeding cars in a way that made me feel faint.

"Mrs. Cheever kept us late," Angela was saying in her soft, breathy voice. "She reminds me of this awful teacher I had when I was at school at Monteverde. She would never let us get up until she had finished talking and then she just went on and on forever until you could have screamed."

"You were at Monteverde? In Gstaad?" asked Wyndy. "A coincidence incredible! I was there, too. At St. Etienne'"

"Oh, I knew a boy at St. Etienne's," she squealed. "Did you know Bobby Harris?"

"I wasn't there long enough to get to know anybody," he said.

"What did they throw you out for?"

"Drinking champagne in my room. Well, it was my birthday, for Pete's sake."

"I know. Schools are so stuffy," said Angela. "I was at Monteverde almost until Thanksgiving, but then they caught me climbing the fence one night. I was only going to meet Bobby, but you would have thought it was a federal crime the way they carried on. They didn't want a person to have any friends."

"Those boarding schools are back in the Dark Ages," Wyndy agreed. "The brown-varnished halls, the comical plumbing, the laughable heating system and that inevitable awful pot of honey on the dining-room table getting brown and crusty—I was never so glad to get thrown out of a place in my life."

He reflected a moment. "I was thrown out of Hargrove Academy in Sussex once, but that wasn't half as much fun. At St. Etienne's they yelled a lot and tore their hair. It had its funny side. But at Hargrove it was just a lot of old guys standing around looking grave and saying they were disappointed in you. No spectacle. No excitement."

"I've never been thrown out of a British school," said Angela, interested. "What did you do?"

"Threw a plate through the dining-hall window. The food was awful. Boiled cabbage night after night. And let me tell you, all that stuff you hear about freedom of expression being guaranteed in England is a lie. All I did was make that little protest with the plate and I was out on my ear. After that, I told Sally, no more boarding schools. I won't go. You no sooner get used to the place than they throw you out."

"The more schools you get thrown out of, the harder it is to get in another one anyway," said Angela, sounding a practical note.

These two were obviously soul mates. Never having been thrown out of anything, I was completely left out of the conversation. Not that it mattered. As far as they were concerned I was invisible, even though, scrunched up as I was behind the stick shift, I somewhat blocked their view of each other. I was glad to see Burger Heaven coming into view ahead. While this little chat had been illuminating, explaining, for example, why Sally hadn't put Wyndy into a private school, I did not want to spend any more time listening to reminiscences of Wyndy's and Angela's colorful pasts. I was ready for lunch.

Wyndy pulled up into a parking place near the door. "Here we are. Why don't you go inside, Jessica, and stretch your legs? Angela and I will just go through the drive-in window and eat in the car. I'll honk the horn when we're ready to go."

I could take a hint. They wanted to be alone. Angela got out so I could clamber out over her seat, and I went on inside. The beauty of being in the familiar, air-conditioned interior of Burger Heaven, savoring the delicate smell of grilling hamburgers and french fries, compensated me at once for all the hardships of my journey.

"Jess!" someone called.

I looked behind me and saw that Marian was sitting in a booth by herself. As soon as I got my hamburger, I joined her. "Who did you get a ride with?" I asked as I slid into the booth.

"I'm giving Kim Kirk five dollars a week to give me a ride," she said. "What about you?"

"Wyndy let me come with him."

She looked around. "Where is he?"

"He's going through the drive-in window. He and Angela are going to eat outside and honk for me when they're ready to go."

"I call that interesting," said Marian. "What's this Angela like?"

I unwrapped my burger. "She seems nice enough. She's kind of sweet."

"I wonder why people say she's wild?" Marian said, narrowing her eyes. "I bet there's a story behind it. Why didn't the Harpers like her? That's what I ask myself."

"She doesn't seem wild to me," I said, taking a healthy bite out of my hamburger.

"You know what my mother says?" Marian went on. "She says boys may go out with wild girls but they don't marry them. This superficial, flashy attraction isn't so important in the long run."

"In the long run nothing's important," I said. "In the long run we're all dead."

"You sure are in a bad mood today. Honestly, a person can't say anything!"

I wasn't overly cheerful, it was true. I had realized that I wouldn't mind having some of that superficial, flashy attraction that Angela had. It would be kind of fun to have boys falling all over themselves to impress me.

"Marian, tell me the truth. What do you think I ought to do with my hair?"

"Get a permanent," she said. "Mine's great. I don't have to do a thing to it. I just wash it and shake it out and that's all there is to it. It's the only way to go."

I eyed Marian's frizzy hair uneasily. "Maybe so," I said. "I just can't quite seem to make up my mind to do it."

I was only halfway finished with my fries when I heard the honk of the Hirondelle's horn. I jumped up, leaving my tray on the table, and dashed out because something told me that if I were slow getting out to the car, Wyndy's response was *not* going to be "*Cara mia*, you are worth waiting for."

Angela smiled sweetly as she got out to let me clamber into my place behind the gearshift. "You had the right idea, Jessica, to go inside where there's air-conditioning. It's so hot out here."

Wyndy shot her a reproachful glance. "Beautiful one, you mean to tell me you think air-conditioning is better than me beside you holding your hand?"

"That was nice, too." Angela smiled, lifting her hand to her hair to check and see if her braids were still properly in place. Her fingers were covered with antique-looking rings. She even wore a ring on her thumb, a chunky topaz. "Wyndy tells me you're a sophomore. How do you like Senior High so far?"

"Okay," I said, cautiously tucking my feet farther up under me as Wyndy shifted down for a stoplight.

"You should try going to a few stuffy boarding schools, Jessica," said Wyndy. "Then you'd really appreciate Senior High. Heck, at Senior High it's fun just looking around at all

the types. Did you see that guy yesterday in the swimsuit and
dinner jacket? The American sense of humor—I love it!''

"That was Andy Cooper," said Angela. "I went out with
him for a while. He is so funny."

"Don't say that," said Wyndy, turning a corner sharply. "It
drives me mad with jealousy. Next thing you know I'll be
sticking a dagger into this Andy."

Angela looked pleased.

"Who's the black guy," Wyndy asked, "about six foot four
with a gold earring in one ear?"

"I guess you mean Reggie Kearney. Don't try sticking a
dagger into Reggie," said Angela. "He'd cream you."

"Wyndy's not afraid," I put in. "He was almost kidnapped
at gunpoint a while ago and it didn't bother him a bit."

"Kidnapped!" exclaimed Angela, her eyes growing round.

"It was nothing," said Wyndy.

"Why would anybody want to kidnap you, Wyndham?"

"The streets of Rome are full of senseless violence," he said
with a careless wave of the hand.

"Like New York, I guess," said Angela.

"No comparison," said Wyndy, looking annoyed.

"I've never been to Rome," said Angela. "It sounds nice.
Why did you leave?"

"You're forgetting the senseless violence in the streets," I
said wryly.

Wyndy gave me a sidelong glance. "Jessica hates to eat in the
cafeteria," he said.

I could take a hint. He wanted me to shut up. I perceived that
Wyndy was one of those tiresome people who always have to be
in control. He had planned a flirtation full of *"cara mia's"* and
soulful looks and he didn't want me messing up his game plan
by comments that might distract Angela from the main issue—namely him and her.

"I guess the girls in Pine Falls must seem pretty dull to you
after the ones you've known in Rome," said Angela, looking
at him from under her eyelashes.

"I'm enchanted by the girls in Pine Falls," he said. "One of
them in particular."

"You're just saying that," said Angela.

Wyndy cast her a smoldering look.

"The light is green," I pointed out.

My head snapped back as we took off in a burst of speed. I couldn't decide which was the more disgusting, Angela's appetite for flattery or Wyndy's willingness to lay it on. Between all that and the excessive speed of the Hirondelle, I was glad when we got back to the school parking lot.

Angela got out of the car first. "It was nice to meet you, Jessica," she said softly. "I hope it wasn't too uncomfortable there behind the gearshift. I'd be happy to take a turn there myself but I'm afraid my legs are too long."

Wyndy closed his door and cast an openly appreciative look at Angela's long legs.

I said, "Three in front makes a pretty tight squeeze." The fact was that I was of mixed mind whether to pass up Wyndy's offer of a ride tomorrow and take my chances at the cafeteria. Riding over the gearshift was not turning out to be my idea of fun and I was already asking myself if yesterday's meat loaf had not been, perhaps, an isolated incident.

"Oh, you're not in the way at all," said Angela. "Is she, Wyndy? I'm *glad* you can come along."

The funny thing was, I was sure she meant it. As I made my way back to class, leaving Wyndy whispering in Angela's ear, it occurred to me that Angela probably got a certain kick out of having a witness to Wyndy's endearments. I expect she was hoping I'd go around telling everybody how crazy he was about her. She was probably one of those very insecure people that needed other people to be telling them all the time how great they were.

I got to enjoy the benefits of the Hirondelle again that afternoon. I had to admit it was nice not to have to ride home in the hot, noisy school bus. The speed of the Hirondelle wasn't so bad once you got used to it. And since we were only going home, I didn't have to bother about my hair and could just let the wind whip through it, which was nice. The only bad part of the ride was that I had to listen to Wyndy's lecture.

"Jessica," he said, "do me a favor and don't go talking to Angela about my family and so forth. When you've moved around a little bit the way I have you'll find out that there's nothing that bores people so much as talking about people and places they've never seen and that they're never going to see."

"What should I talk about, then?" I asked.

He raised an eyebrow at me pointedly.

"You want me to keep quiet, huh?"

"Now you've got it. I'm *happy* to give you a ride to lunch. But I don't want you getting in the way when I'm making my move on Angela. Understand?"

"I can take a hint. Maybe I'd better just eat in the cafeteria."

"Nah, if you come down sick from the food, it'd be on my conscience. Besides, it's okay. Angela likes having you along."

"I think she does. Funny, isn't it?"

"She likes an audience," he said.

I got out of the car at home feeling as if I had a lot to think about. My personal experience with romance was very limited. Unless you counted the time Wally Hankin had tried to kiss me in the fifth grade and I had given him a black eye, I hadn't actually had a romance yet. But I had done some reading on it, and somehow I had definitely come away with the impression that three was a crowd. Yet Angela liked an audience. I was beginning to suspect that real life romance was somewhat more complicated than my reading had led me to expect.

When we got home, Wyndy changed right away and went out jogging. I was made of different stuff. My one thought was to get something cold to drink and something fattening to eat to rebuild my strength before tackling the mountain of homework I had been assigned.

"I found a wonderful Italian grocery in Raleigh," Mom announced cheerfully when I went into the kitchen. "I stocked up on prosciutto and finoccuona sausage. I thought it might help Wyndy feel more at home."

I did not know what prosciutto or finoccuona sausage were, but I didn't like the sound of them. I dipped myself some ice cream without comment and sat down to eat it. Mom pulled up a chair across from me. "Tell me the truth, Jess," she said. "How do you think Wyndy's adjusting to school?"

"Like a fish to water," I said promptly. "*I'm* the one with the problems."

"But sugar, you've lived in Pine Falls your entire life. You know everybody. I don't think you realize how difficult this must be for Wyndy."

I looked glumly at my ice cream. If Senior High was difficult for Wyndy he was hiding it very well. I debated about whether to fill Mom in on my problems with snobby seniors, the school cafeteria, my loneliness for Audrey, and my indecision about whether I should get a body wave or not, but before I had the chance to say a word she went right on talking about Wyndy's problems.

"I don't like to say this about Sally," Mom said, "but I'm beginning to think she may not be the best parent in the world. We haven't heard a word from her since Wyndy arrived and we don't have any idea where she is. Suppose something had happened to Wyndy! She wouldn't even have known."

"You don't think she's left him here for good, do you?" I asked. Wyndy as a permanent fixture in the household didn't bear thinking about.

Mom smiled. "Of course not," she said. "And for that matter, I suppose in any real emergency we could probably get in touch with some representative of the family by going through the New York office of Sarto Motors. It's just odd, that's all. If you had gone flying off to Italy all by yourself, you can be sure your father and I would have wanted you to phone or cable that you had arrived safely."

"She probably knows he can take care of himself." I ate a spoonful of ice cream thoughtfully. "He can, too," I added.

Mom's brow was furrowed. "She's so casual about him. When I think of how we spent an entire day together in New York and she never mentioned him...."

"He probably just didn't come up," I said.

"Well, I mentioned you. I don't like to be one of those boring women who goes on and on about her children, but naturally I ended up talking about you now and then.'' Mom really looked upset. I guess it was hard to come down from thinking that Sally Sarto was wonderful to thinking that she was an awful mother. "Your father and I are afraid that Wyndy has been neglected," she went on. "Oh, not in the material ways, of course, but missing out on the real closeness to his parents that he should have had. We're going to try to spend plenty of time with him. Your dad's going to offer to take him fishing Saturday."

"But I thought Dad was going to work Saturday. He always works on Saturday."

"He thinks he can get away this Saturday. Some things are more important than money, sugar. If Dad has to hire another man part-time in order to spend more time with Wyndy we think it will be well worth it."

I almost choked on my ice cream. What about all that stuff I used to hear about how a small business couldn't make a go of it if the owner only put in a forty-hour week? What about how we all had to make sacrifices to keep More and More Mufflers out of the red? Why, when Dad was first getting the business off the ground, he had even missed my piano recital! It seemed to me that Wyndy was getting all the advantages of being in our family without having to make any sort of contribution at all.

"Is something wrong, Jess?" asked Mom.

"Must have choked on a crumb," I said, coughing.

"Don't be silly," she said. "There aren't any crumbs in ice cream. If you're feeling resentful of Wyndy, just come right out and say so."

"Okay, I feel resentful of Wyndy. There."

"I'm disappointed in you, Jess."

"Mom, have you ever heard of the cowbird?" I said.

"I thought we were talking about Wyndy."

"We are. A cowbird is a bird that goes around laying its egg in other birds' nests and when the baby cowbird hatches it's bigger and stronger and nastier than the baby birds that really belong in the nest and it gets all the food."

She followed my gaze to the fridge. "Sweetheart, we don't have to have prosciutto every night. Look, I understand what you're saying. You're afraid that Daddy and I won't love you as much now that Wyndy is here, but that's not true. Believe me, we have enough love in our hearts for both of you."

I couldn't bring myself to say any more. Instead, after I finished my ice cream, I went quietly to my room and to relieve my feelings began typing out the rough draft of my horror story. In my present mood, the story went very fast. I saw at once where I could find the glamorous sort of creepiness, the emotionally riveting center that my story needed. Right in my own house, that was where.

The villain could be a young Italian exchange student. After further thought, though, I crossed out "Italian." If my story won the contest, I didn't want the Friends of Italy and the Italian Anti-Defamation League picketing my house. Better make him a Transylvanian exchange student. I bit my lip with intense concentration. He was beautifully dressed, in gorgeous pastel shirts and white linen pants, he drove a snazzy yellow sports car, had sleek dark hair, black lashes, striking dark brows, and only the closest observation showed that his teeth were slightly wolfish. He was going to have to have sharp teeth since he spent his evenings sucking the blood of young girls. It was a traditional story but with a new twist.

Down the hall I heard the shower turn on full force in the bathroom. Wyndy was back from his jogging and was now using his usual sixty gallons of hot water. I guessed I would have to put off washing my hair until the next day.

"It was a dark and stormy night," I typed. Then I crossed it out. A bit trite, that dark and stormy night. I tried another tack. "The branches of the tall oak tree beat against the windows of the gym. As the wind rose a few drops of rain rattled against the roof." That was better. I would have the lights go out at the school's autumn dance and the first victim would be found slumped against the folded-up gym mats. The trick was to sort of intermingle the creepy stuff with the ordinary everyday things that everyone could recognize.

I lost all sense of time as I worked on my story until suddenly Mom knocked on my door and asked me to come help set the table for dinner. "I think it's wonderful the way you buckled down to your homework right away," she said as I followed her to the kitchen. "So organized." I blushed.

Wyndy sauntered out of his room, dressed now in a shirt of shocking tangerine paired with pants in dull old gold, a color scheme that might have been all the rage in Tanzania but was quite unusual in Pine Falls. I had noticed by now that two or three outfits a day were standard for him. He liked fresh clothes after his afternoon shower. But even as extensive a wardrobe as his was apparently beginning to feel the strain because as Mom and I were gathering up the plates and silverware, he leaned against the frame of the kitchen door and asked, "Do you know a really reliable laundress, Mrs. MacAlister?"

"Goodness, Wyndy," said Mom, "I'm not even sure there are any laundresses in Pine Falls."

"A reliable laundry, then? What do you do about your clothes?"

"We wash them ourselves," said Mom. "I hate doing laundry. I'd rather cook. So everybody takes care of their own things. Jess, take Wyndy to the laundry room and show him how to work the washer and dryer. I'll set the table for you."

"This way," I said. I led him to the little room off the kitchen where the washer, dryer, clothespins and laundry baskets lived in an atmosphere of warmth and lint. I could tell this was going to have to be basic instruction, so I began by opening the washing mashine.

He peered into it, eyeing the agitator mistrustfully.

"You put the clothes in here," I explained. "Put the soap in first, though. I'll show you how to measure it in a minute. This is the bleach dispenser. You pour the bleach right in here and it comes out during the wash. That way there's not so much risk of the bleach making spots on the clothes."

"Spots?" he said, growing pale. "This black thing, what's it for?"

"That's the agitator." I explained. "It goes round and round during the wash and churns the clothes up. That part's automatic. You don't have to do anything to it. Now up here are the various cycle indicators.''

''But doesn't that agitator thing chew up the clothes?''

''If you have something really delicate you wash it by hand, of course.''

''Che?''

''I mean you sort of swish it out in the bathroom sink and let it drip dry in the bathtub.''

I must admit I enjoyed initiating Wyndy into the mysteries of doing laundry. The laundry room was the only place I had seen yet where he was totally out of his depth. However, my smug smile was wiped off my face later that night when I went in to take my bath and had to make my way through a forest of pants and shirts hanging from the shower curtain rod. He had obviously decided he didn't trust the washing machine

My bare toes stepped into a cold puddle where the shirts had dripped on the bathroom floor. I pushed a handful of clothes on hangers to the back of the curtain rod with a clatter and was promptly hit in the face by one that leapt off the rod. Disentangling myself as well as I could from the shirt that was lying like a sack over my head, and its hanger, now somehow entangling my arm, I almost lost my footing on the slippery floor and had to grab onto the towel rack to steady myself.

After I finished my bath, I went back into my room and worked on my story. It was therapeutic. My home life might be deteriorating fast, but my story was making solid progress. I put into it all the anger I felt toward Wyndy and just kept writing until I felt better.

When I rode to lunch with Angela and Wyndy the next day I made good use of the time by jotting down notes on their conversation. That would be handy, I figured, for writing the dialogue when the villain was luring innocent young girls to their death behind the gym mats. Wyndy was laying on the flattery very heavily and it all had a lovely, swarmy, insincere quality that would suit my villain perfectly.

''Your eyes are amazing, Angela,'' he said. ''They have this incredible clear blue color like the sky in warm climates. I've never seen anything like it.''

Angela glowed self-consciously as I jotted down a few notes on a tiny pad of paper. They weren't paying any attention to me anyway.

"Oh, I'll bet you say that to all the girls," she said.

"No, honestly, how could I? Your eyes are something special. Have you ever thought about being a model?"

"Oh, I don't think I'm pretty enough for that. Do you?"

"No question of it. You really ought to think about it. No, I take that back. Don't start thinking about going away from here to be a model. I want you right here in the Hirondelle with me," he said with a charming smile. I noted it all down, adding the charming smile in parentheses.

That night I had very little homework so I was able to finish roughing in the rest of my story. It was shaping up well. I read over what I had done so far with deep satisfaction. Then, when I had finished my writing for the night, I collected my old terry-cloth robe and went into the bathroom to wash my hair.

Wyndy's clothes still festooned the bathroom, which made the process of washing my hair fairly difficult. Not only was the water tepid and fast turning cold, but it was hard for me to keep from splattering shampoo all over the shirts.

Nobody was happier than I when the next day Wyndy found a nice Puerto Rican laundress, Manuela, who worked for Angela's family, to take care of his laundry. Manuela came that afternoon in her tiny little car and collected every stitch Wyndy had worn so far. Then her little car tooled away with its back seat piled high with crumpled heaps of Italian shirts and pants and white laundry bags full of underwear and socks. After she'd driven away I breathed a sigh of relief. It was going to be lovely to brush my teeth without lifting wet socks out of the basin, delightful to take a bath without first making my way through a forest of dripping shirts. In principle, I was opposed to people paying other people to wait on them, but my principles had crumbled fast when my bathroom was invaded by rows of dripping shirts.

Judging from the quantity of clothes that had been carted away, I wouldn't have been surprised if Wyndy had been reduced to wearing nothing but his black silk bathrobe, but I misjudged him. He had plenty of clothes in reserve and continued to look perfectly turned out for every occasion. When he and Dad set off for fishing on Saturday morning, Dad looked predictably comic in a beat-up old hat with fishing lures stuck in it, his nut-brown hair sticking out from a hole in the hat back and his stomach straining against his old red-checked shirt. Wyndy, however, was wearing a black-striped fisherman's jersey over formfitting jeans that tapered down to pale ankles and beautiful blue canvas shoes. Watching them go off together was like watching a big shaggy sheepdog set off with a Doberman pinscher.

"Did you remember the mosquito repellent?" called Mom as they headed out to the car.

"I remembered it," said Dad. "I remembered it."

"What about the Band-Aids?" she called after them.

I heard Dad snarl before he revved up the engine and drove away.

I spent my Saturday next door helping Peter with a series of ambitious photos of Susannah Simmons.

Just before supper, Wyndy and Dad returned victorious, carrying a string of fish. Wyndy immediately vanished into the bathroom for a good long hot shower before his date with Angela.

I heard Mom's voice from the kitchen. "Jessica!" she called.

She looked up when I appeared at the kitchen door. "I'm going to need some help cleaning these fish, sugar."

I could hear the sound of the shower in the background.

"Mom," I said, "do you think we could get an auxiliary hot water tank or something?"

She looked up at me vaguely. "Are you running short of hot water, dear? I'll try to remember to turn the thermostat a little higher." She lowered her voice confidentially. "I think Wyndy and your dad had a nice talk."

"Super," I said. I looked at the string of fish spread out on the counter. "Well, that makes it all worthwhile, doesn't it?"

Chapter Five

As the weeks passed and I kept riding to Burger Heaven with Wyndy and Angela, I got to the point where I was almost sorry to see Marian there. Lately, she had gone completely overboard on gossip.

"Guess what I heard," she said as soon as I sat down. "I heard that Angela got thrown out of boarding school when she was only thirteen. Over a boy!"

"These rumors are usually awfully exaggerated." I carefully removed the pickle from my hamburger. "It's terrible the way people gossip."

"Awful," agreed Marian perfunctorily. "By the way, Angela and Wyndham have really got something going, haven't they?"

"They do seem to go everywhere together," I agreed.

"I wonder what on earth he sees in her?" said Marian, looking at me pointedly.

"She's very nice, actually," I said.

Marian knew very well that nobody was in a better position to tell her about the progress of Wyndy's and Angela's relationship than I was. After all, I sat between them twice a day on the way back and forth from lunch. But I would have felt awful talking about them. After all, they *were* giving me a ride.

And Marian would probably have been disappointed in my information anyway, because whatever was going on between Angela and Wyndy, I did not think it was scandalous.

A few minutes later I heard Wyndy honking and I had to jump up, leaving Marian to brood alone over her hamburger about ways and means of expanding her information network.

Outside, I clambered into the Hirondelle and we sped out of the parking lot.

"Baby Day is coming up pretty soon," Wyndy commented as he turned onto the highway. "I saw some posters in the hall about it."

Baby Day was a subject that I really felt strongly about, but because of my agreement with Wyndy that I was going to keep quiet during our lunch expeditions, I said nothing.

"Yes," said Angela softly. "It is. I guess you're more used to girls with brown eyes, aren't you?"

He looked at her, startled, no doubt trying to figure out the connection between Baby Day and brown eyes. What he didn't seem to realize was that in Angela's mind every subject led to a compliment for her. If it didn't, she considered it a dead bore.

"Blue eyes are the prettiest, *mia bella*," he said, a bit absentmindedly. "Blue eyes like yours. What are you going to wear for Baby Day, Jessica?"

"Me?" I said, affecting surprise. "Were you addressing me?"

He glared at me. "Sure, I was talking to you. Angela and I can't be in Baby Day. We're juniors."

"Well, I'm not going to be in Baby Day either," I said, "as it happens."

"The senior class is giving a nice prize for the best costume," Angela pointed out. "I think you'd be a really cute baby, Jessica. Maybe you'd win. Last year, Tom Jenkins won. He wore the sweetest bonnet with lace on it and everything. And a giant baby-blue romper suit. He even had a pacifier."

"The problem with being small like me," I said, "is that if I dressed in rompers and sucked on a pacifier it might be a little *too* convincing. What if they demoted me to kindergarten?"

"Don't be ridiculous," said Wyndy, glancing at me. "Nobody could confuse you with a baby."

It was gratifying that Wyndy was looking at me for the first time—or would have been had I not been so sure he was mentally measuring me for rompers.

"If you're so interested in Baby Day," I told him, "why don't you see if you can get to be an honorary sophomore or something and be in it yourself?"

His eyes laughed. "Beneath my dignity," he said.

"Mine, too," I said curtly.

"I can see why you say that," he said. "Not everybody's cup of tea, Baby Day. Would it be okay if I brought a camera and took pictures? Would anybody care?"

"Collecting examples of American humor?" I asked crossly.

"Yup. Besides Baby Day is sort of a quaint custom. Like the wassail bowl in England."

"The sooner it's stamped out the better," I muttered.

By now I was no longer taking notes on the line Wyndy was handing Angela. For one thing, the juice seemed to be trickling out of his line. It didn't have quite the zest and the sickeningly overdone character it had had at first. And for another thing, my horror story was finished so I didn't need any more dialogue for it. I had about decided it was as good as I could make it. The time had come to mail it in.

"Now don't forget my party tonight," Angela was saying. "You come, too, Jessica. There won't be any other sophomores there, but you won't mind that, will you?"

"Gee, I'd love to, Angela," I said. "But I'm working on a special project tonight. Karen is coming over to help me."

"Bring Karen, too," said Angela.

"I think I'd better get this work done," I said.

"Well, if you change your mind, come on over."

I couldn't imagine how Angela found the time to have parties the way she did. It seemed to me that now that I was in

Senior High I was busy all the time. On top of all my home-work, I had my special projects.

That night Wyndy left for Angela's party and I finished typing my horror story. I put a fortune in postage on it and dropped it in the blue mailbox a couple of blocks down from our house. I spent a few happy moments thinking of what I could do with three hundred dollars if I won first prize, then I turned toward home and started thinking of my other pressing task—Project Help Stamp Out Baby Day.

At eight, Karen came over to the house as we'd planned to help me make some posters to put up at school. When she came in, I was down on the floor with sheets of poster board and a heap of colored markers.

"Where's Wyndham?" she asked.

"Over at Angela's. She's having a party. Probably her parents are out of town."

"Her parents are out of town and she's having a party?" said Karen, her eyes widening.

"Now, don't go saying anything to Marian," I warned. "Wyndy says Angela just gets lonely because her parents are away so much, so she has all these kids over. That's all. Nothing wild." I held up a poster. "Okay, now look at this one. What do you think?"

My sign said, Interested in Human Dignity? Come to a Meeting in A-106, Monday at Three-Fifteen.

She looked at it. "It's not very exciting, but I guess it's not a very exciting subject."

"Sure it is. We just need to work on it some more." I looked at the poster critically and uncapped a red marker. "Let's ask ourselves what Tom Paine would have done with this poster."

"Who's he?"

"He wrote propaganda for the American side in the Revolution."

"I've never heard of him."

"The American side won, didn't it? That speaks for itself."

"Well, what *would* he have done with this poster?"

"I know." I sketched out a plan on a sheet of notebook paper with my marker. "See, we put a really big FREEDOM in red over the face of the poster. That will get their attention."

"SEX would be better," said Karen.

"We don't want to attract kinks to the meeting," I said. "We want a serious bunch. Now, we'll put a screaming eagle over here in the corner." I roughed it in with a few lines. "And then down here we print the information—what the meeting's about, when, where, and so forth."

"What if the seniors just tear our signs down?"

"Seniors don't read the posters in the halls," I said. "They think they already know everything that's worth knowing."

"I hope you're right. It would be awful if some of those sophbusters showed up at the meeting."

As my chief henchman, Karen had certain drawbacks. She was short on confidence, for example. But she had one important virtue. It turned out she could draw a terrific screaming eagle. We ended up making four brightly colored posters. We decided to put them up in A Building since everybody had to go there for assembly, detention, and hall passes, so they were more likely to see it. We had set our meeting for the Monday after Baby Day. I figured indignation about senior privileges would be at a peak then, and also lots of people could see our posters in A Building as they were coming out of the Baby Day assembly.

I was really excited about the possibilities of my campaign. Maybe I could be the one to change the face of Senior High, the one to make the school safe for sophomores, the one who really made a difference. And now that I had my horror story in the mail, I was able to devote a lot more thought to my equality campaign. In fact, I was thinking about it night and day.

The day before Baby Day, I rode to lunch with Wyndy and Angela as usual. When I went inside Burger Heaven, I saw that Karen was sitting with Marian. As soon as I got my hamburger I went over to join them.

"Has Jess told you about our campaign to stomp out senior privileges?" Karen was saying to Marian. "We've got all these posters made up telling people about our first meeting. Isn't it exciting?'' She bounced a little in her seat.

"It'll never work," said Marian. "You know how stodgy everybody in Pine Falls is. Nothing has changed around here since the bustle went out."

I unwrapped my burger. "Naturally, we've got to *make* it work," I said. "Nothing ever changes if everybody just sits around on their hands. Come to our meeting, Marian. Stamp out senior privileges. Make this a better world!"

"I can't," said Marian. "I'm too busy."

Karen and I looked at each other.

"Oh, come on, Marian," said Karen. "It won't take long. We're just going to meet for a little while after school Monday."

"I never get involved in lost causes," said Marian. She went on talking, as usual, about who was going with whom and why. This was followed by a short discussion of who had broken up with whom and why. Nothing was more interesting to Marian than other people's love lives. Finally, however, she ran out of things to say.

"Golly, it's terrific to be eating real food again," Karen said, gobbling up her last french fry. "The cafeteria food was so bad I had to start taking my lunch, and I was getting awfully tired of peanut butter and jelly."

Marian took a last swig of her milk shake. "Kim's leaving," she said. "We'd better go."

The two of them jumped up and followed Kim out to the parking lot. The burger place, in fact, was emptying fast, and Wyndy still hadn't honked for me. I looked at my watch, feeling uneasy. Could I have missed hearing the honk? It didn't seem likely. The Hirondelle horn was very loud. Angela and Wyndy must have forgotten about me and driven off without me. I jumped up out of my seat, wondering if a taxi would take an I.O.U. and dashed out to the almost empty parking lot. I saw the Hirondelle parked in the shade of a tree. Angela and Wyndy were sitting in it, lost in earnest conversation. They had obviously lost track of time and had not even noticed all the other cars pulling out of the lot.

"Wyndy!" I called plaintively. "Isn't it time to go?"

He looked at his watch with a horrified expression and immediately switched on the engine and revved it up. A few seconds later I hopped in and we were speeding toward the school. But no amount of speeding could get us back on time. We all had to go to the office for late slips and were condemned to detention hall that afternoon.

"I'm so sorry," Angela whimpered as we were leaving the office with our little yellow slips. "It's all my fault."

"Nah," said Wyndy. "It's just one of those things. Maybe we ought to treat Jessica to lunch tomorrow, though. It wasn't *her* fault."

"Oh, I'm so sorry, Jessica," said Angela. "It's all my fault."

"Will you *quit* saying it's all your fault?" said Wyndy.

"Don't worry about it," I said. "So, what's a little detention hall?" I had more important things to worry about—such as Baby Day.

As we all streamed into asssembly on Baby Day Friday I realized more forcefully than ever that I had a long way to go in educating my public. Mac MacInroe walked by me wearing a yellow and blue beanie and with a yellow felt ducky emblem sewn over the alligator on his shirt. Behind him was Holly, dressed in white socks, a skirt ten inches above her knees and with a great big floppy pink bow in her hair. She was carrying her old teddy bear, Bennington. He had a disdainful expression on his threadbare face and seemed to be the only one in this appalling situation who was maintaining his dignity. Bottles, pacifiers, teddy bears, and giant lollipops were everywhere around me, and the number of girls who had turned out to be willing to go to school in flannel nightgowns and slippers positively amazed me.

Inside the auditorium where all the babies were lining up to parade across the stage there was a good deal of confusion. The senior homerooms were going wild waving Sophbuster signs and posters.

Suddenly the pep band let loose a rousing volley of trumpets and everybody cheered. Then sophomores began parading across the stage in bunches, dragging their teddy bears and licking at their all-day lollipops. The Baby Day assembly had officially begun. Peter was standing just below the stage popping flashbulbs at the babies as they passed. It looked to me as if he were just out of flash range and I was tempted to go remind him to move up closer, but then I recalled that it was best, after all, if this event were *not* immortalized on film.

I was shocked to spot Karen. I only saw her for a second, waving a bottle over her head. Then I lost her in the crowd of kids moving across the stage. I covered my eyes. I had no idea that she planned to be a baby. It didn't seem like a very good start to our campaign.

When all the sophomore participants had walked across there was a wait for a few minutes while the panel of judges deliberated. A volley of trumpets burst out amid some confused cheers. Then the president of the senior class led Sam Waterhouse out on stage and awarded him first prize. I had to admit Sam had done a good job of making himself look like a first grader—particularly considering that he had the handicap of being almost six feet tall. He had blacked out his two front teeth so it looked as if they were missing, he was wearing a beanie with a propeller on top, plus short pants, and he was carrying a book bag. But others had done almost as well with the basic costume.

After assembly, in spite of all the confusion, I managed to find Karen in the hall.

"Karen!" I said fiercely, putting a hand on her shoulder. "What do you mean going around with that teddy bear and the bottle?"

She gave me a nervous look. "Uh, I think we ought to try to understand the enemy's point of view, Jess. With me joining in, you see, I can get a better idea of what all is really involved."

I sighed as she disappeared into the crowd. I could see I had my work cut out for me. Even my own right-hand woman was not ideologically pure.

That afternoon after school Wyndy told me he thought he had got some good shots of the cutest babies.

"Where were you?" I asked. "I didn't see you taking pictures."

"Behind stage on the wings," he said. "I wanted close-ups. I got the prizewinner to pose for me afterward. It'll be a nice souvenir of my stay in the States."

Trust Wyndy, I thought, to get better pictures than Peter without half trying. It was impossible to imagine Wyndy forgetting to put film in the camera or standing just out of flash range. He was too efficient.

I sighed, imagining him at some sophisticated ski resort in Austria or someplace, sitting around the fire with other members of the jet set and passing around snapshots of his stay in the U.S.—snapshots of giant babies. You would think the kids in Pine Falls would be more concerned about their world image.

That set me to wondering exactly when Wyndy would be jetting off. We had heard absolutely nothing from Sally since the phone call with the bad connection in which she told Mom Wyndy was on the way. And that had been weeks ago. In the past month or so since then, we had gotten awfully used to having Wyndy around. He was practically a member of the family. And still there had been no word from his parents. I wished I knew how long an expedition to the Himalayas took. I also wished I knew whether Sally's group planned just to walk up and down a mountain or whether they were going to go off looking for the Abominable Snowman. It was unsettling not knowing what was going on or when Wyndy would be leaving.

When we got in from school, Mom called to us from the kitchen. "Letter for you, Wyndy. On the entrance hall table."

I peered over his shoulder as he reached for it. An Italian stamp was on it and the handwriting on the envelope looked foreign.

He tore it open. "It's from Ferreti."

"News from home?"

"Guess so."

He scanned it quickly. "Consuela's twins have cut their first teeth. Ferreti has beaten Mario at ten straight games of backgammon. The weather is unseasonably hot. They hope this letter is finding me well. Consuela sends her regards and warns me not to eat too much American fast food because it is bad for the digestion.''

"That's nice," I said. "Nice to hear from them, I mean. Does the staff all stay at your house even when nobody's there?''

"Yes," he said, looking at me as if I had just come into focus. "Giovanni will never close the house. It belonged to my grandmother Sarto.''

"I guess it must be a big place.''

"I suppose so." A half smile played across his face. "It's not too practical. Hard to heat. It's got a big round staircase winding through it and in the center a round *salóne* with tall ceilings like a church. There are lots of bedrooms—tiny ones, each of them on a different level so you have to get to them by going up and down these crazy little steps. The only big room, really, besides the *salóne* is Giovanni's. That's right at the top with the garden outside. The garden's on different levels, too, like the house—it's terraced and has an old fountain and gigantic twisted wisteria and a view of all Rome lying spread out at your feet." He was looking into the distance as if he could see it. "All Rome," he said, "in a golden haze in the distance, with windows flashing gold along the Tiber.''

"I guess you're homesick," I said.

He shrugged.

Mom came out of the kitchen, drying her hands on her apron. "News from home?" she asked.

"A letter from Ferreti," he explained.

"No bad news, then, anyway.''

"No, everything's fine.''

Mom's bright smile didn't dim and I suppose only someone who knew her as well as I did could see that she thought it was sad that nobody but the chauffeur had written to Wyndy. I suppose I must have felt a teensy bit sorry for Wyndy myself. It wouldn't have killed his parents to drop him a line.

The following Monday was the day of our meeting about senior privileges. Karen and I waited some time in room A-110 for the crowds of indignant sophomores we hoped would help with our campaign. Unfortunately, our meeting was rather poorly attended. The only people who showed up were two boys who had thought the sign was about starting an ROTC program at Senior High—and Wyndy.

He leaned back in the teacher's chair, propping his legs on her desk and waited while I explained to the two boys with the short haircuts that the eagle on the sign was purely decorative and that the meeting was really about abolishing senior privileges. After they had slunk off I confronted Wyndy. I was not in the world's best mood.

"Are you interested in doing away with senior privileges?" I asked.

"Of course," he said, widening his eyes.

Karen was slumped in a desk in a discouraged attitude. "Maybe we should give up," she whimpered.

"I have not yet begun to fight," I said.

"My," said Wyndy, "that has a familiar sound! Did you remember to put an announcement of the meeting in the school bulletin?"

"No," said Karen. "Maybe *that's* where we went wrong. We should have put the meeting in the bulletin."

I threw myself into a desk. "There's a lot of apathy around this place."

"Then we give up?" asked Karen, looking more cheerful.

"No!" I said.

"I only thought . . . if nobody's really interested . . ."

"We need to educate them," I said.

"But if nobody will come around to hear what we've got to say," said Karen, "I don't see what we can do about it. It's just hopeless."

"I don't think it matters whether people *listen* or not," I said slowly, "as long as you say it often enough. We need to drill it into their minds without their consciously realizing it."

"I don't see what you mean," she said. "If they don't listen, they can't hear, right?"

"Wrong," I said. "Subliminal suggestion. That's what we need."

"Hold up a minute," said Wyndy. "I just need to look that up in my English-Italian dictionary."

"Subliminal suggestion is very simple," I said. "If people *hear* something they can be affected by it even if they think they aren't listening. Suppose, for example, I sneaked up on you while you were asleep every night and whispered in your ear, 'Buy soap.' Chances are the next thing you knew you'd be going out to buy soap. That's how it works."

"Ingenious," said Wyndy, looking at me admiringly.

"Jessica's really smart," said Karen.

"All right," said Wyndy, "what's the plan? Tape recorders hidden in two thousand bedrooms, all of them murmuring 'Stomp out senior privileges'?"

"Easier than that," I said, compressing my lips. "All I need is to get control of the mimeograph machine."

"I don't follow you," said Karen.

"You *did* say 'get control of the mimeograph machine'?" said Wyndy.

"Right," I said. "Listen now, think about it a minute. The mimeograph machine is the seat of power in this school. Why does everybody troop down to the office to get a medication authorization form if they need to take medicine? Because the mimeograph machine tells them to. Why, there probably wouldn't even *be* any medication authorization forms if the mimeograph machine didn't churn them out! The mimeograph machine is the root of it all. I need to *get at that machine*. I want every day's announcements to contain a message that will help people see how stupid and unfair senior privileges are."

"How are you going to manage it?" asked Wyndy.

"I haven't quite worked that out yet," I said. "But I can find a way. I don't think many people really realize the subversive possibilities of a mimeograph machine. Nobody's guarding the thing."

"Yeah," Karen said, her eyes lighting up, "maybe you could break into the office at night with a flashlight and just type in some extra lines on the day's announcements. It would be easy."

"I don't think I'd try that," said Wyndy, his eyes laughing. "I hear the American police are very efficient."

It was certainly provoking to have Wyndy sprawled there laughing at me. I did my best to ignore him.

"I'm going to watch for my chance," I said. "Maybe I'll go to the office and tell them I have a burning desire to make myself useful around there. After that, it would be easy to get control of the machine." I got up.

"Need a ride home, Karen?" asked Wyndy, lazily unfolding himself as he rose.

"Gee, thanks, Wyndham," she said. "That would be super! But I thought you just had two seats in your car."

"Jessica can squeeze in behind the gearshift," he said. "She's used to it."

It was true. My toes had a permanent crimp in them from being squeezed under me and sat on.

As we drove home, I did my best to conceal it from Wyndy and Karen, but I had found it deeply discouraging that nobody had shown up for our meeting. It was hard to escape the feeling that this was not my day. In fact, this might not be my year.

This feeling was strongly reinforced when we got home. Sensing activity back by Peter's grape arbor I climbed over the fence as usual to see if there was anything I could do to help out.

Peter had his camera attached to a tripod and was standing behind it with his legs spread out and his eyes screwed up, totally involved in taking the photograph. I glanced over at the grape arbor and was surprised to see that Angela was the day's subject. When she spotted me she jumped up and waved.

"Jessica!" she squealed. "What a nice surprise!"

I pushed my hair out of my eyes and managed a smile. "Hi, Angela," I said. Another blonde, I thought. And I had to admit that Angela was a lot better looking than Peter's usual subjects. She really did have a lovely face. No wonder Peter was enchanted.

"I just popped over to see if you needed any help," I said.

"No, thank you," said Peter firmly. "I don't need a thing."

"Don't you want me to stand by to help clean up? You can just yell when you need me."

"No," he said. "You run along. I can manage."

I looked at him incredulously. He was telling me to get lost. It wasn't so much the words as the tone which loudly said Buzz Off.

"Oh. Well, all right. I guess I'll just be on my way."

Angela gave me another cheery wave as I climbed back over the fence. "See you later," she said.

I banged my knee on the fence as I clambered over it. I was having a little trouble seeing what I was doing with the tears welling up in my eyes, but I stumbled away, wiping my tears with the sleeve of my shirt. I wanted to get past the fence and the trees that separated our lots and out of Peter's sight. Nobody loved me. My anti-senior privileges campaign was a failure. I was a dismal flop. I wasn't even a blonde! I sniffled and wiped away a few more tears.

I didn't want Mom to see me crying so instead of going inside, I sat down on the cold flagstones of our terrace with my back against the terrace wall. I could cry there in peace.

Unfortunately, at that moment Wyndy suddenly came out the back door and saw me. "Something wrong?" he asked.

I sniffled. "I banged my knee on the fence."

He glanced at my knee. "Very delicate things, knees."

"Yes," I said, wiping a tear away.

"Look, I'm sorry I teased you about your campaign," he said. "It's a good idea. It just needs a little time to catch on, that's all."

"It's not just that," I said, my voice breaking.

He knelt down next to me. "What's wrong?"

"Oh, nothing really. Only I think this is the end of a nice platonic friendship."

He looked over the fence. "That fellow next door been giving you a hard time?"

"Not really. I guess he just doesn't need my help anymore."

"Oh."

"I just wish I were a blonde!" I cried.

Wyndy laughed. "Who edged you out with him?"

I shrugged. "Nobody in particular. But with Peter it's always a blonde," I said. "Cheerleaders, majorettes, homecoming queens—you know."

"I think I get the picture. He goes for flashy types. No discrimination."

Since Peter appeared to go for exactly the same type that Wyndy himself did, I didn't think much of his analysis, but considering the touchiness of the situation, I thought it best not to point that out.

"I guess that's it," I said.

"All you need to do is catch his attention."

I looked at him indignantly. "I live right next door. It's not as if he doesn't know I'm alive, you know."

"Catch his attention as a girl, I mean. Lay on that extra flash that catches the eye."

"I guess you think I need a complete make-over. Like those people in magazines where they do Before and After pictures." Wyndy was rejecting me, that was it. After all, I already knew he didn't admire my style. I remembered the way he had looked at my old blue scarf. He probably *pitied* me, for goodness' sake. Well, who could blame him? I wiped my eyes with my sleeve.

"No way," he said. "I think you're perfect just the way you are. I thought we were talking about this fellow next door who likes blondes."

I turned my streaked face up to him. "Do you really, honestly think there's even the remotest chance that if I jazzed myself up a little Peter might take an interest in me?"

"Sure!"

"I don't know," I said. "I'll think about it."

Wyndy, who had been down on one knee beside me, got up and dusted off his pants. No doubt he regretted letting the delicate material grate against the flagstone. "It's probably not worth the trouble, anyway," he said. "Do you really want some guy with a cheerleader fixation?"

"Peter doesn't have a cheerleader fixation!" I said indignantly. "He's just totally absorbed in his art. As an artist he sees everything through the lens of a camera so naturally he's attracted to photogenic types."

Wyndy's eyes laughed at me. "Sure," he said.

After Wyndy had gone back inside, I sat for a while longer on the cold flagstone thinking. I told myself I was utterly disgusted with the way Peter was mooning after Angela. I was well out of it. Who needed Peter anyway? I had my anti-senior privileges campaign to keep me busy. It was going to be a big job requiring a lot of energy. Probably it was just as well that Peter didn't want me around anymore.

After a few minutes I scrambled up, thinking in spite of myself how satisfying it would be to have Peter trailing after me, to have him looking at me with that same besotted look he had fixed on Angela. And maybe there was a chance of its happening, too. He was certainly not going to get anywhere with Angela. Angela was all tied up with Wyndy and besides she was older than Peter. She would ignore him and when he came around nursing a broken heart, I would be there to pick up the pieces. Not the old, humble me, but a new, flashy-style me, a dazzling version of me that would rock him back on his heels and make him *grateful* that I even threw a smile at him.

Maybe I *would* just ask Wyndy for a few suggestions. After all, say what you would about Wyndy, he certainly understood good looks. What did I have to lose?

Chapter Six

Cut off my hair!" I screeched. "You mean cut it all off? I'd look like a boy!"

Wyndy looked me up and down critically. "Get outa here. Nothing could make you look like a boy."

"But girls don't wear their hair short in Pine Falls. It's one thing to see that kind of thing in a magazine and it's something else to go to school that way. People would think I was strange."

"You want to get attention, don't you?"

"I don't know," I said hesitantly. I hadn't realized when I sought Wyndy's advice about jazzing myself up that his ideas would be so *radical*.

"It wouldn't hurt you to lose ten pounds either."

I was indignant. "I'm not a bit overweight!"

"Don't get me wrong," he said, holding up an eloquent hand. "I myself admire a womanly figure. I only thought you told me this Fields guy went in for bones."

It was undeniable that the girls who modeled for Peter tended to have knobby elbows and distinctly countable ribs.

"But I don't *want* to be bony," I said.

"Good grief, Jess. Ten pounds isn't going to make you bony. It'll just point up your cheekbones, define your face a little."

"I refuse to starve myself."

"Exercise is what you need," he said. "You should come jogging with me. By the way, do you play tennis?"

"Very badly."

"Jogging will have to do, then. When you get in shape you'll feel better, get some self-confidence. Believe me, you'll see a difference. Ever worked out with weights?"

"No. And I don't intend to, either."

"Look, do you want my advice or not?"

"I want your advice in moderation."

I was to think of these famous last words the next day, after I got back from the beauty shop. There was a cold draft on my neck, on my ears, and on my forehead. I was afraid to look in the mirror. But I realized I had certainly solved the problem of my hair. Now I hardly had enough hair left to worry about. It was cut short, sleek and close to my head all around except on top, where it was longer, and in front, where there was a little flip of a half bang. It was so short there was a question about whether I would even have to *comb* it.

"Perfect," said Wyndy. "Mousse should keep that little bang in place." He strode into my room and flung my closet open. "Now to work on your clothes," he said.

"I know I need a new look," I said. "But keep in mind I have a limited budget."

He looked at me as if he didn't know what "budget" meant. Very possibly it was a new word for him.

"How much do you have to spend?" he asked me.

When I told him the full amount of my clothing allowance until Christmas he blinked but only said, "Fine. Hand it over to me. I've got to drive to Raleigh this week to get the Hirondelle looked at and while I'm there I'll pick up your clothes. What size do you wear?"

"A six," I muttered. I did not like people to know that it was sometimes possible for me to find my size in the children's department. "But look here, do you mean you're going to spend my entire clothes budget and I won't even get to pick out the clothes or try them on?"

He cast a critical eye at me standing there in my blue skirt and my white, easy-care shirt. "You'd just slow me down, Jess, standing there chirping about how they don't wear that kind of thing in Pine Falls."

"But what if I don't like what you get? What if it doesn't fit?"

He waved my objection aside with a graceful gesture. "So we take it back. No problem. Don't worry, though. You'll like the stuff all right. I have a great eye for a bargain."

I threw myself down in my desk chair. "I don't know. Maybe I should just change one little thing at a time. Why go overboard?"

"Trust me," he said. "We'll have that Fields guy eating out of your hand."

"I'm not so sure this is going to work out."

He looked over at my dressing table. "Is that your makeup?"

"Well, yes. The light is so much better here than in the bathroom that I always put it on in here."

"You need more of it. I can see that."

"What do you know about makeup?"

"I know that Sally's got pounds and pounds of the stuff and her worst enemy would have to admit she looks great."

"I don't want to look overdone." I had the feeling that what would be suitable makeup for a middle-aged member of the jet set would not be at all the sort of thing I should wear.

"You want to get this guy's attention, don't you?" He looked at my face thoughtfully. "I'd say that you want lots and lots of whatever that stuff is girls put on their eyes."

"What stuff? Mascara? Eye shadow? Highlighter? Eyeliner? What do you have in mind?"

"I don't know. You'll have to work out the details. Just lots of eye junk. That should do it."

I looked in the mirror. Maybe Wyndy was right. Maybe I did need more eye junk. I was going to have to work myself up to it, though. There was only so much change a human being could take at one time without showing signs of strain.

Luckily for me, the next morning a cold front moved in. That meant I was able to wear the hood of my parka up much of the day. I was having a hard time facing the fact that the world was going to have to see me sooner or later without my hair and the parka hood gave me a little time to adjust. I let it down in homeroom, though and when Karen turned around to ask me a question her mouth moved but no sounds came out for a minute. Finally, almost choking, she cried, "Jess! Your hair! What did you do to it?"

I quickly flipped up the hood of my parka again. "I just got a haircut," I said.

"Let me see it," Karen said. "It's cute. I was just surprised, that's all." She regarded me with clinical interest. "It's cute, but it needs something. I don't know what."

Mrs. Grooms said, "Class, I have just a few announcements." She picked up a one-inch sheaf of announcements and began placidly working her way through them.

"Students who would be willing to give up their study hall in order to work as a volunteer in the school office should apply to Miss Dixon at the office," she finished.

Karen nudged me with her foot. I saw just what she meant. Opportunity was knocking! Here was my chance to seize control of the mimeograph machine! I was so excited I let my parka hood slip off my head again. My hair was sparse and sleek enough now that it took a major effort of will to keep the hood up anyway.

Unaware of the momentous development, Mrs. Grooms smiled and dropped the announcements in the trash. The bell rang and I jumped up. I could dash down to the office and apply for the job right now. It would make a good first impression to be eager. Furthermore, maybe it would give me a tactical advantage to be first.

Luckily, my homeroom was in the main building so it didn't take me long to get to the office. I popped in and stood in front of the counter wishing I had worn high heels to school so as to look taller and more mature. Finally, I managed to catch the eye of a vague-looking, middle-aged woman with overpermed hair.

"I've come about the volunteer work for the office," I piped up. "You know, the volunteer position that was mentioned in the announcements this morning? I'm the student who is willing to give up her study hall to work in the office."

"Yes," she said, her eyes wandering to the window. "We're really overloaded here. We need some help with the filing." She looked back at me. "Do you type?"

"Forty-five words a minute," I said.

"That's good because we could use some help with the typing, too."

"Let me write my name down here for you. I can start tomorrow. My study hall is fifth period."

"That's good," she said vaguely. "We've got a lot of work piled up around here. Boxes in the back piled up almost to the ceiling, letters that need to be typed. . . ."

"Mimeograph machines that need operating," I put in.

"I usually do the mimeograph machine myself," she said. "It's delicate. It's better if the same person does it all the time."

"Nasty, messy things, mimeograph machines."

She contemplated her fingers thoughtfully. "I do sometimes spill that fluid on me," she admitted.

I had to hurry out of the office and run to make it to my next class and even so I slid in just after the tardy bell, but it was worth it. I figured it wouldn't be long before I had my hands on the mimeograph machine. The reins of power at Senior High were almost in my hands. My moment had come.

"How was school, sugar?" said Mom. "And why on earth are you eating ice cream wearing your parka?"

"School was fine," I said. "I think I'm about to have a breakthrough in my campaign against senior privileges. The parka is to cover up my new haircut."

Mom dimpled. "It can't be that bad. Let me see."

Mom had been working on the church's fall festival until all hours the night before and had slept late that morning so she hadn't seen me in all my glory at breakfast.

Wordlessly I dropped the hood of the parka. "My goodness," she said. "It is short."

"Told you," I said.

"Don't worry, sugar, it will grow back."

I heard the front door swing shut and Dad came in the kitchen door. "I must have left those invoices at home," he said. "Susan, can you help me look for them?" Suddenly, he caught sight of me and stopped in his tracks.

"I got a new haircut," I said.

"I can see that," he said. "What did you do to make them so mad at you?"

"Richard!" Mom said. "Don't tease her. It may be a little on the short side, but after all, it will grow."

"It's a new look," I said. "I figure it should hit Pine Falls in the year 2000."

"Until then, if I were you I'd invest in some hats," said Dad. "Come on, Susan. I've got to get back to the shop. I think they must be somewhere back in the bedroom. I've already searched the car from top to bottom."

"Did you look under the seats?" asked Mom as they headed for the bedroom.

I stood in the kitchen doorway and craned my neck to get a glimpse of myself in the living-room mirror. My hair didn't look so bad, really. It was kind of cute. It just needed getting used to. The funny thing was, the more Mom and Dad criticized it, the more I could feel my conviction growing that it was just the kind of haircut I needed. I had learned from experience that if Mom and Dad thought something looked sweet the chances were it was hopelessly old-fashioned. They were twenty years behind the times. I decided the haircut was probably okay. All I needed to do was to lay on some more eye makeup and maybe wear some gold hoop earrings. I would look less bare that way.

I returned to my ice cream, now fast getting soupy. I had only taken two bites, however, when Wyndy came up behind me and swept it away.

"Tut, tut, Jess," he said. "It's not ice-cream time. It's jogging time."

I saw that he was already dressed in white shorts, a cotton sweater and his jogging shoes. His smooth dark hair was, I realized, somewhat longer than mine.

"I don't want to jog," I said. "It's cold out there."

"Not when you've run a few miles," he said. "You get nice and warm then."

I don't know exactly how it happened, but somehow I ended up going jogging with Wyndy in spite of the fact that it was the last thing I wanted to do. I did remember to put on a knitted cap to protect my practically bare head from the cold, which was a good thing because outside a wind was blowing.

"This is a terrific place to jog," Wyndy said. "One of the great things about Pine Falls is there's practically no air pollution."

"You mean that golden haze over Rome that you're always talking about is just pollution?"

He grinned. "I guess so."

I could feel the pavement meeting the balls of my feet with a rude thud at every jog I took. "You're really not too crazy about Pine Falls, though, are you?" I said.

"You're wrong about that. I like it a lot. It's a pretty little town and I think Senior High is hilarious...." He smiled a little. "I mean, I think it's very entertaining. Also I really like Richard and Susan."

One of the more crushing developments in the past weeks had been that Mom and Dad had actually asked Wyndy to call them by their first names. It was just another example of how people's principles tended to crumble when Wyndy was around.

I didn't say anything else for a while. I was working too hard on breathing. "Don't you think maybe we've done enough of this jogging?" I gasped.

"We've just got started."

"But I can hardly breathe!"

"No pain, no gain, Jess," he said. "Keep going."

A few minutes later he glanced at me. "Maybe we'd better swing by the house and drop you off," he said. "You really must be out of shape. You look awful."

When I went in the kitchen, Wyndy was sipping his cappuccino and Dad was immersed in the morning paper. I could hear
Mom rustling around in the laundry room.

"Dad, could you give me part of the paper?" I asked.

"What section do you want, Jess?"

"It doesn't matter. Whichever one you're through with."

He disentangled the front section from the sports page and
handed it across the table to me. "That haircut of yours must
be growing on me. It looks good this morning."

"Thank you," I mumbled, getting the paper unfolded in
front of my face just in time. Dad might be foggy on the question of makeup, but Mom certainly knew a ton of mascara and
eyeshadow when she saw it. I hid behind the front page reading the lead story, "Coed Disappears From State Campus."

I heard Mom's footsteps approaching, then the sound of the
opening of the refrigerator.

"Good morning, sugar," she said. "You're up bright and
early aren't you?"

"Lots to do," I mumbled.

Still pretending to be immersed in the paper I reached out and
snitched half of Wyndy's croissant, which I devoured in privacy behind the newspaper.

"Want some cheese with it?" he murmured silkily.

I held out my hand for the cheese. There was no way I could
get up and get my Rice Krispies without letting Mom see my
face.

"I didn't realize you liked croissants, sugar," said Mom.
"Maybe I'd better double my order with the baker. Isn't it nice
how having Wyndy has broadened all our horizons?"

When Wyndy was ready to leave I cautiously peeked out
from behind my paper, then jumped up and managed to hurry
out the kitchen door while Mom's back was turned. "Good-
bye!" I called over my shoulder.

"Goodbye, kids," Mom called. "Have a good day!"

"What's all this hiding behind that newspaper?" Wyndy said
as we walked out to the car.

"I was afraid Mom was going to think I had on too much eye
makeup."

"I just have to take it easy on my right foot," I panted. "An old horseback riding accident."

My remark did not have quite the effect on Wyndy, however, that I had hoped. "You ride?" he said, lighting up. "Terrific! We'll have to lay our hands on horses and get in some riding."

I was turning pink in the face, but I managed to gasp, "Jogging is better exercise."

"True." He looked at me sympathetically. "Maybe we'd better just walk the rest of the way home."

"I'm fine," I gasped. I had my pride.

When the house at long last came into view, though, it looked wavy, like one of those mirages travelers see in the desert.

"Okay," said Wyndy. "We're home."

I didn't say anything. I didn't have any breath left. I just stood there, bent at the knees and gasping like a goldfish.

He glanced at his watch. "I'll just leave you here and go on. I haven't really been running long enough to get the kinks out."

I nodded mutely and grasped at the porch railing to keep myself from sagging to the ground. I felt as if someone had beaten me all over with an ironing board. As I staggered inside, though, I realized that this little outing had had one advantage. I was back first and if I didn't faint, I would beat Wyndy to having a hot shower.

I woke up the next morning feeling exhausted. As I layered on mascara, eyeliner and three shades of eyeshadow, a vision of Peter formed before me—his sensitive lips, his nicely modeled chin, his soft, bewildered-looking eyes. Was he really worth all this?

I blinked my eyes and my lashes stuck together. I opened them again with an effort to glance at my watch. I was even ahead of schedule. I would have time to go in and have a leisurely breakfast. The only problem was I was afraid Mom might take one look at me and tell me to go back and wash my face.

I saw that he was already dressed in white shorts, a cotton sweater and his jogging shoes. His smooth dark hair was, I realized, somewhat longer than mine.

"I don't want to jog," I said. "It's cold out there."

"Not when you've run a few miles," he said. "You get nice and warm then."

I don't know exactly how it happened, but somehow I ended up going jogging with Wyndy in spite of the fact that it was the last thing I wanted to do. I did remember to put on a knitted cap to protect my practically bare head from the cold, which was a good thing because outside a wind was blowing.

"This is a terrific place to jog," Wyndy said. "One of the great things about Pine Falls is there's practically no air pollution."

"You mean that golden haze over Rome that you're always talking about is just pollution?"

He grinned. "I guess so."

I could feel the pavement meeting the balls of my feet with a rude thud at every jog I took. "You're really not too crazy about Pine Falls, though, are you?" I said.

"You're wrong about that. I like it a lot. It's a pretty little town and I think Senior High is hilarious...." He smiled a little. "I mean, I think it's very entertaining. Also I really like Richard and Susan."

One of the more crushing developments in the past weeks had been that Mom and Dad had actually asked Wyndy to call them by their first names. It was just another example of how people's principles tended to crumble when Wyndy was around.

I didn't say anything else for a while. I was working too hard on breathing. "Don't you think maybe we've done enough of this jogging?" I gasped.

"We've just got started."

"But I can hardly breathe!"

"No pain, no gain, Jess," he said. "Keep going."

A few minutes later he glanced at me. "Maybe we'd better swing by the house and drop you off," he said. "You really must be out of shape. You look awful."

Wordlessly I dropped the hood of the parka. "My goodness," she said. "It is short."

"Told you," I said.

"Don't worry, sugar, it will grow back."

I heard the front door swing shut and Dad came in the kitchen door. "I must have left those invoices at home," he said. "Susan, can you help me look for them?" Suddenly, he caught sight of me and stopped in his tracks.

"I got a new haircut," I said.

"I can see that," he said. "What did you do to make them so mad at you?"

"Richard!" Mom said. "Don't tease her. It may be a little on the short side, but after all, it will grow."

"It's a new look," I said. "I figure it should hit Pine Falls in the year 2000."

"Until then, if I were you I'd invest in some hats," said Dad. "Come on, Susan. I've got to get back to the shop. I think they must be somewhere back in the bedroom. I've already searched the car from top to bottom."

"Did you look under the seats?" asked Mom as they headed for the bedroom.

I stood in the kitchen doorway and craned my neck to get a glimpse of myself in the living-room mirror. My hair didn't look so bad, really. It was kind of cute. It just needed getting used to. The funny thing was, the more Mom and Dad criticized it, the more I could feel my conviction growing that it was just the kind of haircut I needed. I had learned from experience that if Mom and Dad thought something looked sweet the chances were it was hopelessly old-fashioned. They were twenty years behind the times. I decided the haircut was probably okay. All I needed to do was to lay on some more eye makeup and maybe wear some gold hoop earrings. I would look less bare that way.

I returned to my ice cream, now fast getting soupy. I had only taken two bites, however, when Wyndy came up behind me and swept it away.

"Tut, tut, Jess," he said. "It's not ice-cream time. It's jogging time."

"Let me see," he said, putting his hand on my chin and turning my face toward him. He looked at me critically. "Can you blink okay?"

"Yes," I said, blinking for him as he opened the car door for me.

"Good." He headed around the car for the drivers seat.

I buckled my seat belt, stretched out my legs luxuriously before me and wiggled my toes as we took off. "Gee, it's nice not to be sitting behind the gearshift."

"Today's your lucky day. You aren't going to have to sit behind the gearshift at lunch either."

"Angela's not coming? Is she sick or something?"

"She's taking a friend of hers to lunch."

I looked at him curiously. "Are you two getting along okay?"

"Sure. You know that nobody could get in a fight with Angela. She'd be apologizing all over the place before you said ten words. But we don't have to go to lunch together every day of the week."

"We'd better eat somewhere besides Burger Heaven, then. If you come inside the place without Angela, Marian's going to be spreading it all over school that you two have broken up."

He looked at me blankly. "Who's Marian?"

"The one-woman news service of Senior High," I explained briefly. "How about Ronnie's? They have good hamburgers."

"I hate to sound un-American, but I'm getting fed up with hamburgers." He looked dreamily into the distance. "What would taste good to me right now would be some nice *fritta di scampi e calamaretti*."

"What's that?"

He lifted one hand as if trying to pluck a translation out of the air. "Oh, you know..." he said. Suddenly he snapped his fingers. "Uh, little octopuses."

"Not at Ronnie's," I said with finality.

He sighed. "Yeah, I know."

A little later, when I got to homeroom, for the first time I faced the world without my parka. It wasn't as bad as I had thought it would be. With all that eye makeup on, it was like wearing a black mask for Halloween. I felt anonymous.

"Boy," said Karen, impressed. "You really look different."

I hoped that was a compliment, and looked around for Peter, anxious to try out my new look on him. I saw no sign of him.

"I wonder where Peter is?" I said. "He doesn't seem to be here today."

"He's at the university hospital having allergy tests," said Karen. "He ought to be back at lunchtime. His mother was telling my mother about it the other day. They test you for hundreds of things there, oak, pollen, sawdust, dog hair, that sort of thing. Then they send you home with a long list of things you're supposed to stay away from."

As soon as the bell rang I jumped up and rushed out. I bumped into Mac right at the doorway—or rather he bumped into me. He seemed to come at me from nowhere and *thwack* my books spilled all over the place.

"Let me get those for you," he said. He gathered them all up and tucked them under his arm. "Gee, I practically ran you down, Jess. I'm sorry. Tell you what. Let me carry your books to your next class."

He was breathing rather heavily on my face.

"That's all right, Mac. I can handle them," I said, reaching for them. "Besides, we're not even going in the same direction."

He cast a disappointed look in my direction as I made my getaway. I had the distinctly odd feeling that good old teddy bear Mac was coming on to me.

At lunchtime, Wyndy and I went to Ronnie's drive-thru window and ate in the car. I took out the cellophane-frilled toothpick and then bit into my bacon, lettuce and tomato sandwich. "It's great not to have to be eating lunch with Marian for a change," I said with a contented sigh.

"She's the one that's always talking about people?"

"That's right."

"Why is this Marian so interested in Angela and me?" Wyndy asked. "Why should she care what we're doing?"

"I think she's attracted to glamour."

He looked amused. "And she thinks we're glamorous?"

I took another bite of sandwich. "I guess so. Of course, she's never waded through your wet socks hanging in the bathroom."

"Funny how everybody loves a star," said Wyndy. "One time I knew this guy—he was good-looking, rich, had a smashing backhand and could do a pretty decent jackknife dive. In other words, your typical, average star. But whenever he started to get close to a girl he'd start telling her his troubles, how insecure he felt and so on and wham, she'd get away so fast you couldn't see her dust. None of them wanted to go out with the ordinary, messy human being, you see. They wanted to go out with the star."

"I think that's terrible!" I said, shocked.

He took a bite of sandwich. "It's natural. Everybody's got troubles of their own. Who needs to hear somebody else's? Tell it to a shrink. They're paid to listen."

"But I don't see how you can be close to somebody unless you know about their troubles," I said stubbornly. "That's what being close is."

To my surprise he reached over and tweaked my nose. "I promise you, Jess," he said, "other people's troubles get old fast."

I fingered my nose uneasily, but refused to be diverted. "Does Angela have a lot of troubles?" I couldn't be sure who he was talking about. Was it him, or Angela, or somebody else entirely?

"Don't we all?" he said. "Look, if you don't want those potato chips, I do."

I pushed them over to him.

"You know, Angela's parents really like me," he said, glancing at me. "And keep in mind it isn't polite to look so surprised when I tell you that."

"I'm not surprised," I said with a guilty start.

"They think I'm a steadying influence on Angela." He demolished three potato chips in a single bite. "Wouldn't be surprised if it put Angela off me altogether the way they carry on about how terrific I am.''

"Oh, dear, I hope not," I said sympathetically.

He shot me an amused look. "You think I couldn't get along without Angela? You're wrong."

I didn't know what I thought. Was it Wyndy who had the boring problems—or Angela? This was a disturbing conversation and I decided to change the subject.

"I don't think about you and Angela at all," I said untruthfully. "My mind is completely occupied with my anti-senior privileges campaign. Today is my first day working at the office, you know. I've got to be figuring out how to get my hands on that mimeograph machine."

He dispatched the rest of the potato chips. "For you, it should be a piece of cake," he said, licking the salt off his fingers. "Say, how does this Fields guy go for the new you?"

"I don't know yet. He's off this morning getting his allergies tested."

Wyndy sniggered.

I shot him a nasty look. "Anybody can have allergies," I said. "It doesn't have anything to do with what a person is like underneath."

"You got me wrong. I'm with you all the way," he said, his eyes crinkling. "What are a few sneezes among friends?"

I felt it was not very nice for Wyndy to sit there looking perfect and laughing at the frailties of others. I turned the conversation to a less touchy subject. "I love fall, don't you?" I said, looking at the sweet gum and apple trees ahead of us, splendid in their color.

"Sure, I love the changing of the seasons," he said agreeably. "Unpacking the rough sweaters and tweeds, the burgundies and rusts and the boots."

"I was talking about leaves, not clothes."

He turned on the ignition. "I happen to enjoy autumn the way city people do."

It was weird. But that was Wyndy. It didn't even bother me much anymore that he never seemed to think like regular people.

Chapter Seven

When I reported to the office for work, Miss Dixon led me to a dusty storage room where boxes were stacked practically to the ceiling and gestured languidly toward them. "We need to open all these boxes of supplies and take them to the storage cabinet where they can be issued to the teachers," she said.

An hour later I stood before her, covered with dust. "Finished already?" she said in surprise. "Goodness. Well, tomorrow we'll have to give you something else to do."

"Good," I muttered. Opening boxes had not been what I had in mind when I'd volunteered.

When I met Wyndy at the car to go home, he stared. "Good grief, Jess. You look as though you'd been rolling around in a dustbin. What have you done to yourself?"

"I've been opening boxes in the office. Boxes of paper clips, boxes of rubber bands." I paused dramatically. "Boxes of *mimeograph paper*." I tried to brush off my pants and got into the car.

He switched on the ignition. "Geez, how can you let your-

self get in that kind of shape? I just hope you're not going to
get that dust all over the car.''

I blew a bit of dust off my nose. ''Can I ask you a personal
question, Wyndy?''

He looked at me warily. ''That depends.''

''Why are you so picky about the way you look?''

He grinned. ''That's easy,'' he said, roaring out of the parking lot. ''If you're as good-looking as I am you've got a re-
sponsibility to your fans. It would be a desecration not to give
it the best you've got. *Capisce?*''

''Baloney.''

''Che?''

''I mean, don't give me that,'' I said crossly. ''You always
start spouting Italian when you're throwing down a line. If you
don't want to give me a straight answer, okay, that's fine. You
don't have to.''

''Okay, well, I don't know why. Why is anybody the way they
are? Why does Andy Cooper come to school rigged out in a
swimsuit and a dinner jacket? Why does Mrs. Grooms wear
those dumb plastic beads of hers? People are just different.
Maybe since I've kicked around a little in lots of different places
I know how important first impressions are. Or maybe part of
it's self-respect. It's what I owe to who I am, follow me? I could
just as well ask you why you don't give a flip about how you
look.''

''I do care about how I look. I'm not ridiculous about it,
that's all. Looks are not that important.''

He lifted an eyebrow ironically. ''Aren't they?''

''Looks are important,'' I amended carefully. ''But they
aren't everything.''

''I never said they were,'' he said mildly.

At suppertime that night I noticed that Mom had put a fresh
white cloth on the table. We all sat at our places waiting for her
to make her entrance with the main course. Finally, she kicked
the kitchen door open, came in carrying a large platter, and set
it with a flourish in the center of the table.

"Fritta di scampi e calamaretti," she said, with obvious pride. "The fish market doesn't get much demand for squid but I put in a special order and they brought it over from the coast."

"Squid?" Yuck. I knew whom I had to blame for this—Wyndy. But when I shot him a black look, I was surprised to see that his eyes were glistening with tears.

I felt like crying myself, but for an entirely different reason. If this was the way the meals were going to be running from now on I wasn't going to have a bit of trouble taking off pounds and pounds. It would be easy.

Luckily, there were some shrimps mixed in with the more sinister fried foods, but scarcely enough to maintain a growing girl. Dad, Mom and Wyndy all ate the squid concoction with great gusto. Meanwhile I tried to fill up on pasta while averting my eyes from the tentacles on the platter and trying not to think about them.

After dinner, I asked Mom if she would mind if I skipped cleaning up. To my surprise, Wyndy offered to help out in my place. I made my way to the living room, where I occupied myself by reading my history assignment. While I was thus engrossed, the phone rang and I heard Mom in the kitchen say, "Sally! How are you? How was the expedition? Oh, that's wonderful. Yes, of course. Wyndy's right here."

My history book slapped shut. Sally Sarto had finally surfaced after all these weeks! Maybe Wyndy would be going home now. Oddly enough I did not feel as cheerful as I would have thought. Maybe it was really true that you could get used to anything. After ages of bathing in tepid water, of never knowing what weird thing was going to show up for dinner and of getting talked into doing things that were totally against my better judgment, like riding in the Hirondelle and getting all my hair cut off—after weeks of all this, I could hardly imagine getting along without Wyndy.

I could hear his voice from the kitchen. "Sally?" he said. "What's up?"

It seemed as if Sally were doing most of the talking. Every now and then Wyndy would make some cryptic remark like "No kidding" or "Sure" or "I see." I could hear every word because the house seemed suddenly silent as Mom and Dad and I held our breath and tried to figure out what was going on. All I could hear was the faint hum of the refrigerator and Wyndy's voice. "Okay, I'll let you know," he said finally. "What's your number? . . . Okay, I'll be in touch."

When I heard the click of the receiver on the phone I gave up any pretense of studying and went over to stand at the open kitchen door. Dad had put down the evening paper and was looking at Wyndy. Mom was standing at the counter holding a plate in midair as if she had been quickfrozen.

"That was Sally," said Wyndy, unnecessarily. "She's in Lucerne at a friend's house and is looking for an apartment. She wants to know when she can expect me."

Suddenly Mom seemed to recollect the plate and set it carefully on the counter.

Nobody said anything for a minute. Then Dad cleared his throat and said, "I guess I'll have to be looking for another fishing buddy, huh?"

"Oh, dear," Mom said, "just when your trunks had arrived and you were all so nicely settled in and everything."

"I can't keep camping on you forever," Wyndy said.

"How can you say that, Wyndy? Why we *love* having you!" Mom said.

"It seems too bad for you to get uprooted in the middle of the school year," Dad suggested hesitantly. "I don't suppose you'd like to ask Sally if you could finish out the year here."

Wyndy looked over at me. I coughed awkwardly. "Uh, do you really want to go to Switzerland?" I asked.

"I can't keep imposing on you," he said.

Mom made an unintelligible distressed noise.

"But we *like* having you," I said. "If you don't want to go, why don't you just tell Sally you want to finish the school year here?"

He looked uncertainly at Mom and Dad.

Mom put her arm around him and kissed him on the cheek.

He brightened a little. "Well, maybe I'll just call Sal and tell her I'm going to stay till the school year's over."

"You don't think she'll mind, do you?" asked Mom.

"Nah," said Wyndy, with a flash of his white teeth. "She's probably already got something else cooking. I'd just be in her way."

"Why don't you call her from our bedroom," suggested Mom. "That way you can have privacy."

Wyndy came back from the bedroom a few minutes later smiling. Mom let out a deep sigh of relief. "Oh, good," she said. "Now we can all relax."

Not really. I had more or less come right out and asked Wyndy to stay on. That bothered me. I guess what upset me as much as anything was having to admit to myself that I was getting fond of him. It was hard to say when I had started to like him. It must have begun so gradually that I didn't even notice, until I realized he might be leaving.

I wasn't entirely happy to recognize the change in our relationship. Getting fond of people is risky. They can let you down. Also, they can not like you quite as much as you like them. Furthermore, they can go back to Rome.

The next morning, on the way to school, Wyndy was in great spirits.

"What this car needs is wings," he whispered. "Do you think if I got her a license plate that said Genie, she'd fly?"

"Why are you whispering?" I said, bending toward him to hear better.

"I don't want to hurt her feelings." A mischievous look came into his eyes. "Hey, want to see a car tap-dance?"

"No!" I thought I had better distract him. "Was Sally surprised that you wanted to stay here?" I asked.

He grinned. "I guess so. Here she'd given me the Hirondelle just to get me to come and now I'm acting as if I like it here."

I looked at him in astonishment. "You mean the Hirondelle was a bribe?"

He reached a hand out the window and patted its smooth yellow surface. "Not bad for a bribe, huh?"

"Sally must have really wanted you to come to North Carolina."

"I guess so. Once she got it into her head that I might be kidnapped in Rome there was no stopping her. How would it have looked in the paper? 'Heir to Sarto Fortune Kidnapped While Father Busy Drying Out and Mother Man-hunting in Himalayas'? Kind of an embarrassing headline."

"You don't really believe that's all she was thinking of!" Sally might have her little faults but I didn't see how she could be Mom's best friend if she were a monster.

He glanced at me. "Nah, Sal loves me, you know. It's just in a way that's hard for other people to see because she's not very motherly." I was relieved to see he had settled down into a reflective mood and that there was no more mention of cars doing tricks. "It was really my *balia*, my nurse, Giulietta, who took care of me when I was little, you see," he said. "Then she went back to Naples because Giovanni said I was starting to talk like a Neopolitan and it was driving him crazy. So then, Miss Drew came. She was a very proper Pennsylvania lady, but Giovanni and Sally undercut her a lot by taking me off skiing and letting me go to their parties and eat food that Miss Drew said was indigestible. It was a nice way to grow up, with champagne mixed with orange juice for breakfast and Miss Drew getting all pink in the face with disapproval. But the upshot of it was that I don't really have a standard mother-son thing with Sally. We're kind of a casual family, I guess you'd say."

"She wasn't very casual about the kidnapping business," I pointed out.

"Well, she might not have been keen to feed me my pablum, but that doesn't mean she wants me shot down in the streets. I think I mentioned that she loves me." He gave me a wry look. "I don't know why I feel as if I sound pathetic explaining that my mother loves me."

"Don't worry about it." I stifled a smile. "It's easy for me to believe that she does." In fact, although I had a hard time understanding why Sally didn't keep in touch, it had never occurred to me that the reason was she didn't love Wyndy. How could anybody not love him? Look how ridiculously fond I had gotten of him myself.

"What you've got to remember," he said, "is that this is a kind of a ... a sticky time for Sally."

"With Giovanni needing a long rest, you mean?" I suggested helpfully.

He reached with some difficulty into his hip pocket and pulled out a thin leather wallet. He tossed it into my lap. I picked it up, not sure what I was expected to do with it. It was still warm from being in his pocket and made of beautiful, supple leather that was lovely to touch.

"Open it." He glanced over at me as he pulled out into the busy traffic of Seventeenth Street.

I opened it and saw that Giovanni's picture was in it. I had no trouble recognizing him because he looked a great deal like Wyndy, but with heavier eyebrows and a more thundery looking face. He was a very good-looking man. "My father," Wyndy said briefly.

"You're very like him," I said.

A sunny smile passed briefly across his face. "Thank you." He concentrated studiously on the traffic, his eyes straight ahead. "He can be a heck of a nice guy, but ..." he hesitated, "sometimes I get to where I can hardly even remember that. Now the sound of his voice on the phone means trouble. His face at the door means trouble. His handwriting on a letter— the same thing. Trouble."

"Maybe he'll get all fixed up," I said, looking at the dark face in the wallet.

"Maybe," he said shortly. He had pulled off Seventeenth Street now and we were getting close to the school. I was sorry because I would have liked to talk more. I felt as if I were really getting to know Wyndy at last.

"So here I am telling you my boring troubles," he said, making a face.

"I don't think they're boring," I said.

We pulled into the juniors' parking lot and I flexed my toes comfortably. They had almost recovered from their permanent crick. "Is Angela coming to lunch today?" I asked.

He lifted both his hands from the wheel in an expansive gesture. "I cannot tell a lie. Angela will be eating lunch with somebody else. Do me a favor and don't mention it to that one-woman news service what's-her-name."

I heard the bell ringing in the distance and should have jumped out of the car with the greatest of speed, but I didn't. "So," I said, "her parents carrying on about how great you were really did put her off you, after all."

"You can't think of any other reason for her to go off me? Very flattering. But think of this—maybe I've gone off her."

"Was that it?" I asked quickly.

"This is a multiple choice test," he said with a mischievous look, "and the final choice is 'all of the above.' No, really, Angela and I are getting along fine and I'm taking her out Saturday night, which makes her parents happy. It's only that she's going to lunch with somebody else now. You should be glad. More room to stretch your tootsies and all."

I wrinkled my brow. "I think I've got it. You and Angela are still dating but you aren't going steady."

"Right. If you've got any other questions at all about my personal life I will be more than happy to fill you in as it's well known that I'm good-natured to a fault," he added.

I was a tiny bit late getting to homeroom, but as I paused a moment outside to collect myself, I reflected that this was not necessarily a bad thing. This was my chance to make a grand entrance. After all, I hadn't spent twenty-five minutes putting on eye makeup that morning in order to sneak around and have nobody notice it. I straightened my shoulders and walked into the class, taking care to bat my eyelashes in the direction of the front-row seat where Peter invariably sat. Mac leaned in my direction and began turning slightly pink, but Peter didn't even look up. It was infuriating. I couldn't stand in the aisle batting my eyelashes forever. Peter had his biology book open on his desk and was staring at it with the intense concentration of somebody who had failed to crack a book for a week and had only just now realized today was test day.

Giving up, I went on back and slid into my usual seat behind Karen as Mrs. Grooms called roll.

"You look great," whispered Karen, turning around while Mrs. Grooms was busy writing on the board. "I love your new look. Have you got to the mimeograph machine yet?"

"Not yet," I said. "But maybe I will today. Last night I looked up a quotation I can put in with the bulletins, just in case I get the chance to slip something in them today."

"Fantastic. Let me see it," she whispered.

I passed up the index card on which I had copied down my quotation. "In the view of the Constitution," it said, "in the eye of the law, there is in this country no superior, dominant, ruling class."

"Give it back now," I whispered. I wanted to bolt out of class the minute the bell rang so I could try to collide with Peter as he went out the door. He was slow moving, and if I were alert I thought I could easily make up the six desk lengths that separated us and manage to bump into him.

"You really think this is going to work?" asked Karen, looking at the index card doubtfully.

"It's a start. It was John Marshall Harlan that said it. I think he was a judge on the Supreme Court."

The bell rang and I tore the index card from Karen's hand and raced for the door. I might have made it, too, if Mac hadn't put his foot out and tripped me. I managed to keep from breaking my ankle by grabbing onto the nearest object, which happened to be Mac himself, and falling into his lap.

He beamed at me. "Gee, Jess, I'm really sorry. You came by so fast I couldn't get my foot out of the way in time." I could feel his warm breath on my ear. It had not seemed like an accident to me, far from it. I gave him a smile that was pretty friendly, considering the circumstances. "That's okay," I said. "No harm done."

Fifth period I showed up at the office to do my volunteer work. A skinny young woman I didn't recognize was sitting at one of the desks typing with two fingers.

I put my books away under the counter. "I'm Jessica MacAlister, the student volunteer," I said. "Where's Miss Dixon?"

"Flu," said the young woman gloomily. "Mrs. Martin's out with it, too." She went on pecking at the typewriter keys, pausing only to mutter under her breath and consult a stack of forms to her right.

"I wonder if I could help out," I said. "I do a little typing."

She jumped out of the chair with alacrity. "You type? Oh, that's great. These things have to be done today and it turns out you can't even make corrections on this ditto paper. I'm the assistant librarian and I said I would help pitch in, but frankly it's just beyond me."

I took her place at the typewriter. After looking at the long lines of x's she had put on the ditto master, I took it out and put in a fresh sheet. "The Art Club will have a meeting Thursday at three-fifteen to discuss the upcoming Art Fair," I typed.

"Oh, you can do it!" she sighed in relief. "That's great. You don't by any chance know how to work a ditto machine do you?"

"No problem," I said blithely. I didn't know how, actually. But surely the thing came with directions.

"That's just great," she said again. "Mr. Sturgess's secretary said she would come show me how this afternoon, but machines just terrify me."

"I've got the whole hour," I said. "I'm sure it'll be no problem at all. I'll take care of it."

"Oh, great, great, great," she said, backing toward the exit. "Maybe I'll just run on back to the library then—if you're sure you can manage." She made a quick getaway.

Left alone I gloated at the ditto sheet in the typewriter. My fingers began to move quickly over the keys as I reflected that Miss Dixon would probably let me take over the job for good. She had not struck me as a glutton for work.

I clattered away on the typewriter. A student came to the counter to ask a question but I didn't even look up. "Miss Dixon and Mrs. Martin are out with the flu," I said. "You'll have to come back Monday."

At last I ripped the last page out of the typewriter and began prowling around the office looking for the mimeograph machine. I soon found it in a little alcove behind the storage closet. Complete working instructions had been laminated on the machine by the manufacturer so all I had to do was follow them carefully. I poured the clear mimeograph fluid into the machine's cylinder until it reached the level marked Full. Then I moved the lever that opened the slot in the machine where I inserted the ditto master and once I had slipped that into its slot I pulled the lever back again. I filled the paper holder with paper. Finally, I pushed the button marked On and the machine began churning out papers with the announcements printed on them in purple.

I was almost finished and everything seemed to be going well, when suddenly for no reason the papers started coming faster and faster. Soon the machine was throwing papers all over the room at a terrific rate. There were papers on the cutting table, papers on the floor. A high-flying sheet of paper hit me in the face before I finally found the button marked Off and cut the blinking thing off. I stood there for a minute breathless, sympathizing with the young librarian's point of view on machines. It was as if the silly thing knew I was up to something and had tried to give the alarm. I began gathering up all the flyaway papers and stuffing them into the wastepaper basket. At least I did have the announcements finished, I thought. And there, right at the bottom, before the announcement of Macaroni and Cheese for Lunch was Justice Harlan's inspiring statement. I swelled with pride. Today hadn't been a total loss after all.

Suddenly I heard a familiar voice calling "Service, please. Look alive there, folks." I stuck my head out and saw Wyndy standing at the counter.

"Wyndy!" I said. "What are you doing here?"

"I have come to check out," he said.

I hastened over to the counter, still holding my precious stack of mimeographed sheets. "What do you mean, you've come to check out?"

He laid a mimeographed form on the countertop. "See here? I have completely fulfilled all the requirements. Please note the names of my parents and the numbers at which they can be reached." He eyed it thoughtfully. "Bit of a high long-distance bill it would be, though. And here on line five is the reason for checking out—family emergency—and the time of checkout—two o'clock."

"What family emergency?"

"Have you forgotten this is the day I have to take the Hirondelle to Raleigh to be checked out?"

"You call that a family emergency?"

"I call the Hirondelle a member of the family. Let's not split hairs over what's an emergency." He looked around the empty office. "Understaffed around here, aren't they?"

"Okay," I said. "Leave it with me. I'll try to figure out where they put these slips."

"Sorry you have to take the bus home today, Jess, but look on the bright side. Tonight I'll be winging my way homeward with your complete new wardrobe."

I had forgotten all about how Wyndy was supposed to buy those clothes for me. "You'll be careful with my money, won't you?" I asked. "I'm not going to get another cent until January. And remember I need a new navy sweater. I've absolutely got to have that. It'll go with everything. You won't forget?"

"You can rely on me *assolutamente*," he said grandly.

He disappeared and I felt fine until I remembered that *assolutamente* he had thrown in at the end. A plain old American "absolutely" would have been more reassuring.

I looked around the office until I found a row of wire baskets. I plopped the still slightly damp stack of mimeographed sheets in the basket marked Announcements. Then I put Wyndy's check-out slip on a spindle labelled Check-out Slips. On second thought I took it off the spindle and carefully smeared his penciled-in name with the heel of my hand. Next I fished a soft drink can out of the wastebasket and dropped a few caramel-colored drops of liquid in a few critical spots like his mother's and father's name. I didn't know how carefully they checked over those slips, but I thought it was probably safer to have it be illegible in a perfectly natural, innocent-looking way. Surveying my handiwork with pride, I replaced it on the spindle. Considering what a blameless life I had led until now, I was very pleased with the aptitude I was showing for a life of crime.

Chapter Eight

Late that afternoon I was sitting in our living room in the midst of a heap of white cardboard boxes that Wyndy had brought from Raleigh strapped on the back of the Hirondelle. I held up a length of purple-and-yellow-striped something or other. "What is this?" I asked helplessly. "Is it a sweater? Or a dress? Or *what*?"

"I guess you'd call it a sweater dress. Notice the matching tights, shoes and hat. Nice, huh?"

"A dress?" I looked at it dubiously. "But it's not much longer than a shirt. What if I have to bend over?"

"That's what the tights are for."

"Purple-and-yellow-striped *tights*?"

"Very chic. It's a casual outfit, but Senior High is a casual place."

"And what is this?"

"Your basic, casual pink suede jacket and skirt."

"The seams are already starting to split." It didn't look as if there were a thing in the entire bunch I could wear. I hoped I was going to be able to take everything back.

"That little split in the front is *supposed* to be there," he said. "It's for allure. It also helps you walk as the skirt is styled kind of narrow. Now this metallic silver shirt goes with it." He held up something gleaming. "Maybe you should get some black tights to go with it. Naturally, you'll push the sleeves up and leave the shirt cuffs unbuttoned. Casual is the look we're after."

"What about the navy sweater?" I asked. "Did you get the navy sweater?"

He fished something dark out of another box. "You won't need that, because I got you this black leather jacket instead."

I began to feel faint. I simply could not see myself in a black leather jacket. "All this stuff must have cost a fortune," I said weakly. "I don't see how you got all these clothes on my budget."

"I told you I had a good eye for a bargain. I found a little-known warehouse where things were being sold for a fraction of their original price."

"Wyndy, you aren't telling me these clothes are *hot*, are you?"

"Hot?"

"Stolen! Because if they are I'm sure they won't let us take them back and we might be accessories after the fact of something, too."

"Of course they're not stolen! They just have imperfections so they're being sold cheap." He held up the suede skirt. "Do you see the slight imperfection in the leather?"

All I saw was an expanse of beautifully soft pink suede, but I had never been able to find those imperfections in the things on the seconds shelf.

"You did save the receipt, didn't you?"

He groped in his pockets. "Must be here somewhere."

I had a cold feeling in the pit of my stomach. "I'm going to have to have that receipt. I just do not have the kind of nerve a person needs to return twelve boxes of clothes without a receipt."

"What's the worry about? Believe me, Jess, once you try them on you're going to fall in love with them."

Suddenly the front door was flung open and Mom staggered in with two bags of groceries. Wyndy moved quickly to her side. "Let me get those for you," he said.

She relinquished them with a smile. "Gallons of milk are so heavy. Would you mind just putting them in the fridge, Wyndy?"

As he disappeared into the kitchen with some of the many gallons of milk we were running through these days since he had moved in with us, Mom drew off her gloves and noticed that I was sitting, stunned, in the midst of the heap of clothes and white boxes.

"Goodness, Jessica!" she said. "What is all that?"

I managed a weak smile. "I've been shopping. Now that I have this new haircut, I decided it was time for a whole new me."

She looked dubiously at the great heap of boxes and the garish clothes spilling out of them. "You must have spent your entire clothing allowance."

"Yup."

"I hope you aren't going to find out later that you need something else when you've already spent your allowance. Did you remember to get that navy-blue sweater you need? The old one is just about shot. I noticed the other day that it was wearing through at the elbows."

"I didn't *exactly* get a navy sweater," I said. "But I got a very basic jacket that I can use instead." I couldn't bring myself to say it was black leather. Mom would think I was joining a motorcycle gang. "It's made out of a very durable material," I added.

Mom picked up the pink suede skirt. "You must have gotten some terrific bargains, sugar. This looks like real leather."

"Seconds," I said. "They all have minute flaws so they were marked down."

"That's good. But remember to look for solid workmanship. You don't want the seams to start splitting before you even wear the things."

"That split is part of the styling, Mom."

She dropped the skirt back into its box. "I'm afraid I don't understand the new fashions. But you always look very sweet." Her eye wandered, as if hypnotized, to the knit thing in broad purple-and-yellow stripes. "And after all, we can only learn from our mistakes. That's why your father and I gave you a clothing allowance in the first place."

I was beginning to wish Mom and Dad were still taking me by the hand and picking out cute little smocked dresses for me the way they did in the good old days when I was three. For the moment my only response was to carry all the clothes back to my room and get them out of sight. That way at least I wouldn't have to listen to Dad's comments on them, which were bound to be more acid than Mom's.

I had no sooner carried away the last box than there was a knock on my door. I opened it cautiously and saw Wyndy standing there looking very pleased with himself. He was wearing a formfitting lilac shirt and crisp cream-colored pants. I found myself wondering how, when he unerringly picked out for himself only the clothes he looked great in, he could come up with such a disastrous collection of things for me. His dark eyelids were half lowered in a lazy smile. "Why don't you try some of them on?" he said. "Which do you think you'll wear to school?"

"I'm going to have to give it a *lot* of thought first," I said in a funereal tone.

He raised a hand as if to ward off my protest. "I know. You want to work out your own style of wearing the things. You don't want me to interfere at the creative stage, right?"

"Something like that."

"The way you tie the belts, the way you turn the collars, that's what really makes it work for you."

I had no idea what he was talking about. All I did with clothes was put them on. I didn't do anything creative with belts and collars. But I certainly didn't want Wyndy fiddling around with my belts so I thought it was better to agree. "Right," I said, closing my bedroom door. I leaned against it, looking at the clothes heaped on my bed. I had the grim but inescapable feeling that I was going to end up wearing them. It was as if I had accidentally gotten on a train and it was too late for me to get off.

Sure enough, while I was laboriously putting on my eye makeup, getting ready for school, I found myself thinking that Wyndy's feelings were going to be hurt if I didn't wear some of the things he had bought. Not to mention that Mom might think it was peculiar if I showed up at breakfast in that old green skirt I'd spilled ink on when she knew I had a closet full of new clothes.

I looked speculatively at the stack of white boxes. Finally I decided that the purple-and-yellow getup at least looked warm, so I fished it out. It was nestled in some tissue paper emblazoned Adolpho's. It was a funny name for a discount warehouse, but I had more pressing matters on my mind than the whims of discounters. I carefully bunched up the tights and slipped my feet into them, then pulled them up. I had to admit that they felt cozy. They were made out of a thin sort of sweater material. I was going to have to be very careful not to snag them. Next I pulled the sweater tunic over my head and pulled its belt tight. Catching a glimpse of myself in the mirror, I was surprised to find that the effect was not all that bad. In fact, that crazy outfit seemed to be just what my haircut and all my eye makeup had needed all the time. I looked at the little matching beret still nestled in the tissue paper. No, enough was enough. I already felt as garishly striped as the caterpillar in *Alice in Wonderland*. I put on the funny little purple slippers that came with the outfit, looked in the mirror, and echoed the caterpillar. "Whooo are *you*?" I asked. I certainly didn't look like Jessica MacAlister, that was for sure.

I flipped my little half bang back in place with my fingers and headed in to breakfast.

"Good God!" said Dad, looking at me with wide eyes.

Mom, who had been occupied flipping over Dad's fried eggs, turned around to see what the fuss was about and was momentarily bereft of speech. "That dress . . . it's awfully short, Jess," she said finally. "Are you sure there isn't a skirt that goes with it or something?"

It occurred to me that this dress had one undoubted advantage. With it on, Mom wasn't even going to notice my eye makeup. I would be able to have Rice Krispies for breakfast. I got my cereal box out of the pantry, then sat down, putting my napkin in my lap with a flourish. There was something about the purple-and-yellow stripes that made me feel like doing everything with a flourish. "It's supposed to be short, Mom. That's what the tights are for."

"Well, this certainly *is* a whole new you, sugar. What do you think, Wyndy? Is this really what kids are wearing these days?"

Wyndy looked at me over the edge of his cup of cappuccino. I couldn't quite fathom his expression. Was it amusement? Or triumph? He put down the cup. "I think it's very photogenic," he said.

Until he said that, I had really forgotten for the moment that the whole point of the new me had been to attract Peter.

"It's certainly very *something* or other," said Dad.

For once, Wyndy and I got away from breakfast early and drove to school going well under the speed limit.

He looked over at me. "So, do you like the outfit?"

"Yup. I had my doubts, I have to admit, but you were right about it. It's terrific when you get it on. I have to hand it to you, when it comes to clothes you're a genius. No question."

"All compliments gratefully accepted."

"What I mean to say is, it must be really hard to picture how things are going to look on people. You know, to tell what would really suit them. I never in a million years would have guessed this was the kind of thing I would look good in. You do think it looks all right on, Wyndy, don't you? Why are you giving me that funny look?"

"I don't know. I feel like I'm sending a sweet little lamb into a den of wolves."

I snorted. "You can't know me very well if you think I'm a little lamb."

"Sorry," he said. "I forgot just for a second there how... uh... fiery you can be."

When we got to school, I tripped out of the car eagerly and headed for A Building. It wasn't that often that we got to school a little early and I couldn't wait to make a grand entrance into the lobby in front of the auditorium where kids gathered before the bell rang.

I opened the glass front doors of the lobby and went in. Only the people nearest me could actually see me. A second later, though, I saw a huge hulk of a fellow bearing in my direction like a bulldozer, the crowd parting before him rather than get trampled. It was Tony Harper and he was soon looming over me with a pronounced leer. However, the expression on his face changed in a comically sudden way when he recognized me. "Jessica!" he said. "You!"

I smiled up at him. "Hi, Tony. Seen Karen around?"

"Jeez, Jess, what have you done to yourself? I didn't even recognize you." He wiped his brow with his hand. "Criminey, here I was barreling over here to get in first with you and...for Pete's sake, why do you have all that stuff all over your eyes? And let me tell you something." He looked at my dress dubiously. "That whatever-it-is is too short. I'm surprised your mother let you out of the house in it."

"I'm perfectly well covered up, Tony," I said. "See the tights?"

I pointed to my toes and held my leg out for him to see. He covered his eyes with one hand. "Holy cow," he said.

"Well, I've got to run," I said blithely. "It's almost time for the bell."

Just then the bell went off with a bone-jangling clamor. I decided to cut around from the outside and go into homeroom by way of the side hall where it would be less crowded.

There was a slight chill against my cheeks as I stepped outside into the morning air, but the rest of me was cozily warm in my sweater outfit.

"Hey!" A boy's voice in the distance floated toward me. I turned to face the long, lanky form of Peter Fields.

"Jess?" he asked in an oddly bewildered voice. "Jessica?"

"Yes," I said patiently.

He shook his head, a bewildered look in his eyes. "I didn't recognize you at first."

I smiled sweetly at him.

He opened the door for me. "Say, Jessica," he said, "I've been thinking . . . how would it be if I took some shots of you? Do you think you could spare me an afternoon? You know, I never noticed those cheekbones of yours before."

I walked through the door with an odd composure. This was the moment I had dreamed of for more than a year. I thought to myself how strange it was to have a dream come true like this—to have Peter saying exactly the things I had always wanted him to say. But even more strange—I wasn't enjoying it. In fact, I felt almost let down. Noticing first that his sneakers were coming untied, I turned to look up at his face with its pink nose and its soft, bewildered eyes and somehow I couldn't remember what I had ever seen in him.

"Well, what do you say?" he asked.

"I don't do modeling."

"It's not exactly modeling. Just sort of posing. I'm only going to take some pictures of you."

I noticed with satisfaction that he had slipped up and said "pictures" instead of "shots."

"No, thank you," I said. "I'd rather not."

Then I fled his surprised face, walking very fast to stay ahead of him. It would be too awful to have to walk next to him all the way to Mrs. Grooms's class. Luckily, where the side hall joined the main hall, I was able to duck in ahead of a crowd of kids so there was no way he could overtake me.

What had made me think I liked him in the first place? He had no sense of humor. How could I not have noticed that before? And he was so klutzy he could hardly find his way out of the rain. I was hit by the awful suspicion that what had attracted me to him in the first place was that he had seemed so helpless. There was no denying that I liked to manage things, and Peter was a guy who just cried out to be managed. It was not very pleasant to conclude that what I had thought was true love was really just my bossy streak. I found myself thinking that all that stuff I had told myself about how Peter was "lost in his art" was not true at all. He was just plain lost, period. His photography was probably just a gimmick to get to know girls. The way he'd chased me down showed that. My cheekbones, ha! As if he could have seen my cheekbones at twenty-five yards! Like Tony, he had just spotted what looked like a smashingly dressed girl and had made for her. Pathetic.

When I reached the door of Mrs. Grooms's homeroom I hesitated a moment. Scanning the classroom, I saw that Mac had strategically positioned himself just two seats behind Karen so that if I sat down in my usual seat he would be right behind me. I made for a seat at the far corner of the classroom. I had to pass a lot of curious stares to get there, but with any luck my sitting there would make me the last person out of the class. That way I wouldn't be likely to run into anyone afterward. That suited me fine. I needed time to think.

After roll, Mrs. Grooms began reading the days announcements but I didn't have to bother to listen. After all, I had typed them all up myself just yesterday. Finally she came to the end of the announcements. "The thought for the day," she read, "is 'In the view of the Constitution, in the eye of the law, there is in this country no superior, dominant, ruling class.' Today's lunch is hot ham spread and cheese."

Karen looked back at me, her eyes gleaming, but no one else seemed to take any notice of the thought for the day. I beamed back at Karen. It was a beginning. My problems with my love life had not, at least, kept me from forging on with my campaign against senior privileges. That was something.

Since Miss Dixon was still out with the flu, I typed up the announcements fifth period as I had before. Then at the conclusion of the bulletins I inserted the day's pithy thought— "Choose equality." Simple and to the point. By itself it didn't seem like much but I reminded myself that by the steady drip of water it was possible to wear away even stone.

After school, I stood by the Hirondelle waiting for Wyndy. Our experiment with the new me had been an incredible success and I wanted to tell him about it.

A few minutes later I saw Wyndy walking Angela to her car at the other end of the lot. The day had warmed up and he had his navy-blue jacket slung over one shoulder. Beside him, silhouetted against the dark jacket, Angela's platinum hair gleamed and glittered in the sun with precisely the same effect that Peter was always trying to achieve with high-voltage lights. I saw Wyndy bend to kiss her on the forehead but they were too far away for me to hear what they were saying.

Wyndy left Angela at her Trans Am and began walking toward me, an elegant, dark-haired figure in the sunshine. He was too far away for me to make out his features, but there was a certain saunter in his step that was unmistakable. I felt I would have known him anywhere just from the way he walked. Around him, cars were already pulling out of their parking places and whizzing out of the lot at dangerous speeds.

A redheaded girl was getting into a little Chevette as he passed. She called to him and he went over to her, his jacket still slung over one shoulder, and inclined his dark head to hear what she was saying. A moment later he waved a casual good-bye to her. As he walked to join me he was grinning. I felt unreasonably annoyed with him. Was it absolutely necessary that he stop to pass the time of day with every pretty girl in the parking lot?

"Who's the redhead?" I asked.

"Ashley Chowning."

If I wanted to find out any more about Ashley Chowning, I was obviously going to have to ask Marian to fill me in because Wyndy clearly had no intention of volunteering any information. I hopped into the car.

Wyndy switched on the ignition and the car's engine leapt to life. "I don't know what it is," he said over the rumble, "but lately I find myself thinking, you know, kind of in spite of myself, that all those sophomores should throw off their chains and all the classes of Senior High should unite in one band of brotherhood arm in arm, shoulder to shoulder. Perfect equality, that's the trick!" He began humming a tune which I think was the Marseillaise, but slightly off-key.

"You noticed my thoughts for the day in the bulletin," I said, unable to conceal my satisfaction. Whatever else should happen, at least it looked as if I were making progress with my campaign to make Senior High safe for sophomores. "Have you heard any of the juniors saying anything about striking down class differences yet?"

"No, I can't say that I have," he said, speeding out of the lot. "It's *got* to work. I'm sure I'm on the right track."

He glanced at my dress. "By the way, how did your day go? The new outfit, I mean. Did you knock 'em dead?"

"It was okay." Somehow I lost my desire to give Wyndy a blow-by-blow account of my experiences with Mac and Peter.

"So it went over the way we thought?"

"Oh, yes." I hesitated. "You could say it exceeded my wildest dreams," I finally said.

"I might say that if I thought in clichés," he replied, sounding annoyed.

"I have no complaints at all," I said. "All is proceeding according to plan." I made a regally dismissive gesture with my hand, then I looked at my hand with surprise and sat on it. If I wasn't careful I was going to end up like Wyndy, with winged hands perpetually making dramatic gestures. "I guess you and Angela will be going out tonight," I said.

"Nope," he said. "I'm going out with Ashley tonight. What about you?"

I realized with chagrin that I had been running away too hard all day to have any chance of being asked out by anybody. Too bad. It would have been very satisfying just then to be able to say I was tied up all weekend. I only wished I had thought of that before I spent so much time avoiding Mac in homeroom and afterward in biology.

"I have a lot of work to do," I said. "I have to research new quotations for my campaign. It's not so easy to find any that are just right."

Suddenly it struck me that Wyndy might be annoyed to hear about the way Tony had swooped down on me in the lobby. It hadn't been part of the plan for Wyndy's own friends to take an interest in me and I intuitively felt he wouldn't like it.

"I was just thinking about Tony," I said. "You should have seen him bearing down on me like a steamroller this morning. It was so funny!"

"Tony!" Wyndy was obviously startled. "He's too old for you. I'll bet Susan wouldn't like you going out with a senior."

I looked at him thoughtfully. "Has anybody ever told you you have a bossy streak?"

He grinned. "Nope. I'm universally admired. Thought you knew that."

After this interchange, I was naturally delighted when a call from Mac came for me that evening. I liked Wyndy to know that he wasn't the only person in the house who got phone calls from members of the opposite sex.

I took the receiver from Dad and perched on the kitchen stool, one leg tucked under me and the other securely twined around the leg of the stool.

"Hullo," I said.

"Jess?" he said. "I've been trying to get hold of you all day. It seemed like whenever I'd just about catch up with you, you'd up and disappear on me."

"Gee, I'm sorry. I didn't realize you were trying to catch up with me. What did you need to talk to me about?"

"Well, actually the thing is I've got these tickets. They're for the *Taming of the Shrew*. You know, the one that's on at the Little Theater. Like I know it's awful short notice and all that but my Mom and Dad just found out yesterday they couldn't go so they gave me their tickets and I sort of wondered if you'd like to go with me, that's all."

"I'd *love* to," I said warmly.

I could hear Mac's breath being slowly exhaled on the other end of the line. "It starts at eight, so I'd better pick you up about seven-thirty so we'll have time to get in and get a good seat."

"Seven-thirty tonight? That sounds good," I said.

"Who was that?" said Dad after I'd hung up and was trying to untangle my legs from the kitchen stool.

"Mac. Mac MacInroe. You know him, Dad."

"The name means nothing to me at all. Did you tell this fellow you were going to go someplace with him at seven-thirty?"

I scrambled down, looking around frantically for reinforcements. "Mo-ther," I called.

She appeared at the door of the laundry room. "What's up, sugar?"

"Mac MacInroe and I are going to go to the Little Theater tonight. He just called me up."

"Isn't this sort of short notice?"

"His parents just found out they can't use their tickets so they gave them to Mac. That's why he couldn't ask me ahead of time."

"A likely story!" snorted Dad.

"Mom, it's a cultural event! It's a Shakespeare play."

I became conscious that Wyndy was standing in the kitchen door, leaning against the door frame. "Sounds like a very thin story to me," he said.

I threw him an indignant glance.

"Quit teasing Jessica, you two," Mom said. "Of course, you can go, sugar. Just be sure you wear something warm. They're predicting frost for tonight."

I flashed her a grateful smile and fled in the direction of my room. I knew just what I would wear—the pink suede outfit with the glittery silver blouse. It might be a little too dazzling for homeroom, but it was perfect for a date. A date! I had a date for tonight! It was hard to remember now how nervous I had been about going to Senior High. Senior High is the only place to be, I told myself. It had everything. Challenges! Excitement! Political intrigues! Boys!

After supper I excused myself promptly and dashed to my room. I knew it would take some time to strip off all my eye makeup and start over again from scratch. Being the new me was a major production. I had no time to waste.

While I was getting dressed, I heard the Hirondelle revving up outside. Wyndy was off for his date with Ashley. A bit later, promptly at seven-thirty our doorbell rang. I blinked my black eyelashes at the mirror in satisfaction. I was ready and I looked smashing.

Feeling it might not be a good thing to leave Mac making conversation with Dad for very long, I dashed out at once. Mac gulped hard when he saw me. I decided that was a good sign.

"I should never have let her get those ears pierced," Dad murmured. "It was downhill from then on."

Mac looked over at him with a startled expression. "Sir?"

"Nothing," said Dad. "Have a good time, kids. And remember to get Jessica home by midnight, Mac."

"No problem, sir," said Mac.

He took my hand and we ran out to his car as it was getting pretty cold and neither of us were wearing coats. As he got in beside me, I flashed him a smile.

"I'm really glad you wanted to go to this thing, Jess," he said. "For a while there I was wondering if you were trying to get away from me. You were pretty hard to get hold of at school."

"Oh, no," I said. "I don't know why you thought that."

He was concentrating hard on his driving. "Just got my license last week," he confided, taking care to come to a full stop at the Stop sign on Maple Street. After looking around very cautiously, he proceeded slowly. "They count off on the test if you don't bring the car to a full stop," he said. "The car's got to stop rolling completely or you're marked off."

"I'll have to remember that," I said. "I'll be taking the test myself one of these days."

Riding in Mac's father's big Oldsmobile was an odd sensation after so many weeks of zipping along in the Hirondelle with Wyndy. A trip with Mac was like driving with Queen Victoria in a state coach—stately, safe, and dignified. I began to relax.

The Taming of the Shrew turned out to be not so bad either once I caught on to the way the people were talking.

After the play, Mac asked me if I'd like to go someplace for a little hot chocolate. Since I didn't have to be home until midnight, that seemed like a good idea. "We could go to Ronnie's," he suggested. "They've got hot chocolate."

I was feeling pretty comfortable with Mac, now. Whatever quality the purple knit dress had that caused him to act strangely, the pink suede suit didn't seem to have it.

It was getting late, but I saw at once that we weren't the only people who had the idea of getting a snack. On the other side of Ronnie's, a parking lot light illuminated the long, yellow flanks of the Hirondelle. Platinum braids gleamed for a second at its window as the girl in the passenger seat shifted her position.

Mac's eyes, like mine, had been drawn to the big, yellow car. "They must be freezing in there," he said, thrusting his hands into his pockets with a shiver. "I wonder why they don't go inside?" As the obvious answer presented itself to him, he flushed darkly.

I am not like Marian, I told myself firmly as we turned to go into Ronnie's. I do not always want to know what is going on with everybody else's love life. But it was odd. It was definitely strange. Why had Wyndy told me he was going out with Ashley when he was really going out with Angela?

Chapter Nine

The following Monday as I stepped in the front door of the school, I passed a couple of senior boys who were earnestly discussing the question of senior privileges. "It's a tradition," one of them was saying. "We don't want to be the ones to break with tradition, that's what I say. The seniors have only got one more year in school. They've been through it all. They deserve to be tops."

"Yeah," a boy in a blue windbreaker was saying, "but the thing is, is it fair? Just because the seniors have been around longer, that's no reason they should get all the privileges. Maybe things should be evened out some more."

The bell rang and I dashed off to homeroom.

People were talking about senior privileges. This was a major breakthrough!

In the afternoon, at fifth period, I went to the office to help out and saw that Miss Dixon was back at work. But even though she was back it seemed to be understood that I was the one who would be doing the daily announcements. I slipped the ditto master into the typewriter and began typing. Typing the long list of announcements more or less took up my whole hour. By having me do the announcements, Miss Dixon saved enough time to have an extra cup of coffee and water the office geraniums. As for me, my mind was on bigger issues. I had decided it was time to quit limiting myself to generalizations about equality and to move on to specifics. The time had come to mention senior privileges directly. It was getting harder and harder to find appropriate quotations. Quotes from the founding fathers and presidents and chief justices were all very well, but none of those guys were directly acquainted with such evils as preferential locker assignments or Baby Day. I was going to have to fashion my own quotes as I strengthened the attack.

That afternoon, when we were driving home after school, I asked Wyndy if he had noticed any more interest in the junior class on the matter of senior privileges.

He answered me rather absently. "I don't think so," he said.

"Well, they either have or they haven't."

"I haven't noticed one way or another," he said.

I looked at him curiously. "Is something on your mind?"

"No," he said, bringing his eyebrows down fiercely.

"Excuse me for living."

"There is nothing, I repeat, nothing on my mind," he said in precisely clipped syllables. "The rest of us are interested in a few things besides senior privileges, Jess. Senior privileges are not that big a deal."

"I'm sorry," I said. "Let's talk about what interests *you* instead."

There was a silence.

"Well?"

"Do you mind, Jessica?" he said. "I just do not feel like talking."

The rest of the trip was spent in silence.

When we pulled up into the driveway, Manuela's tiny little car was parked out in front of the house. She came for Wyndy's laundry on Mondays and Thursdays, but she normally did the pickup and delivery while we were still at school. When we went inside, we found her sitting at the kitchen table with Mom.

"I asked Manuela to sit down and have a cup of tea," Mom explained. "She's pretty upset. Angela is missing."

"Maybe she's out of town with her parents," I suggested.

Manuela shook her head energetically. "No, no! Meester and Meeses Nicholson, they come back last night and she no is there. They call the police."

"She's probably just gone to spend the night at a friend's house and forgot to leave a note," I said.

"She no at school today," said Manuela. "The school say she no there. Mr. Nicholson he call the school."

I looked at Wyndy and he shrugged. "I didn't see her to-day," he said.

"Mr. Nicholson call the police," said Manuela, breaking into sobs. Her thick black hair, coiled up in back, was beginning to slip loose from its moorings and her eyes were red. "They think Miss Angela she is dead."

I sat down suddenly. "The police think Angela is dead?"

"I don't think the police know anything yet," Mom interrupted. "Manuela just means that Angela's parents are naturally very very worried. It hasn't been a week since they discovered the body of that poor girl near the State campus, and State is only about twenty miles away. I can certainly see why Angela's parents are so upset."

"I don't see how she could just disappear," I protested. "Where did she disappear *from*? Who saw her last?"

"It's hard to say," Mom said. "It seems Angela's parents left town Friday night and though there was always someone at the house none of the servants are particularly assigned to keep track of Angela and no one is sure when they last saw her."

"But they must know when she last ate or slept at home," I said.

"The police are probably working on that now," said Mom.

"Miss Angela no eat very much," said Manuela. "She make the sandwich when she have hunger. She eat a little cheese, a little fruit. She make up her bed in the morning. Nobody sure."

I could not believe this was really happening. People did not disappear in Pine Falls. People that I knew did not end up as stories on the front page. There had to have been some mistake. Involuntarily, I looked at Wyndy. This had to be particularly bad for him.

"Oh, I bet she's okay," he said. "You know Angela. She probably just took it in her head to go skiing and forgot to mention it to anybody."

I saw Mom and Manuela exchange a look.

"Her car," I said suddenly. "What about her car?"

"Is all gone," said Manuela. "No car in garage."

"That's good," said Mom. "It's much easier to trace a car than a person." She slid a plate of cookies toward Manuela. "Have a chocolate chip, Manuela, dear. You need to keep up your strength."

The dirgelike atmosphere around the kitchen table was getting to me. I edged my way out of the kitchen and headed back toward my room. Wyndy followed me. I accidentally met his eyes and swallowed hard, not knowing what to say. It was all so awful.

I fled, but he followed me down the hall. "You know, Angela's not a child," he said. "She's old enough to make her own decisions. Her parents ought to get off her case."

I turned to face him. "Wyndy," I said in the patient tones one would use with a kindergartener, "you don't seem to quite grasp that people are afraid Angela has been *murdered*."

"She's okay. She's probably off somewhere having a good time."

Considering that a killer was known to be at large not twenty miles away, this attitude struck me as carefree to the point of being insane. But out of consideration for what I presumed to be his deep, though hidden, feelings, I said nothing.

"Going jogging?" he asked as he turned to go into his room.

"You must be kidding!" I said incredulously. "Angela is missing and you are going *jogging*?"

"I keep telling you she's got to be okay," he said.

As I shut the door to my room behind me I caught a glimpse of myself in the mirror. I scarcely recognized the girl I saw. Not only was she wearing a lumberjack shirt of a vivid, tangerine-colored silk of the sort rarely seen in Pine Falls, but she had large, dark, frightened eyes. I put my hand to my mouth. I *was* frightened.

In the face of this disaster, every other concern seemed to fade away. What did senior privileges matter next to a question of life and death like this? What did it matter that I had been jealous of Angela? Because I realized now that I had been jealous of her, had wanted to be dazzling like her, had wanted Peter and Wyndy to trail after me the way they trailed after her. But now, none of that mattered. Now I only wanted her to be all right.

After a while the four walls of my room seemed to be closing in on me. I threw open the windows to get some fresh air. It didn't seem to help and finally I decided to go out to the backyard. I didn't want to have to go past Mom and Manuela, who were moaning together in the kitchen, so I went out the front door and walked around the side of the house, my feet swishing through the fallen leaves. Down the street, I saw Wyndy jogging away down Oak Street toward Maple.

As I came around the side of the house, I heard the scratching sound of a rake over in the Fieldses' yard. Mrs. Fields was raking the leaves around the grape arbor. She jumped as I approached, then peered uncertainly in my direction.

"It's me, Mrs. Fields," I called, knowing she was a little nearsighted. "Jessica."

"Goodness, Jessica, I almost didn't recognize you. You've done something to your hair. My, don't you look grown-up all of a sudden."

"I guess you've heard about Angela," I said.

She came over to the fence and leaned on her rake. "Oh, my dear, isn't it terrible. My heart goes out to her poor parents. It's just unbelievable. Here in Pine Falls! Why, it's getting to be that no place is safe anymore. Myra Harper told me the police had called over there. Tony used to see a lot of Angela at one time and they wondered if he could give them any lead. It's just terrible. That poor child."

I leaned against the fence. "Have the police talked to Peter?"

"Peter? Why, I don't believe he and Angela know each other too well. Angela's a year older than Peter, you know." She lowered her voice. "And though I don't like to speak unkindly of the poor girl now, I always thought she was a most unsuitable friend for Peter. I remember how the poor Harpers were tearing their hair when Tony was seeing her. It's not the child's fault, of course, but I'm afraid her parents have given her very little supervision, very little supervision at all." She shook her head. "And now we see what it all comes to."

"Some people have the wrong idea about Angela," I said stiffly. "She and I have gotten to know each other pretty well this year and she's really a very nice girl."

"Well, of course, dear, I didn't *mean*..."

"So the police haven't questioned Peter?" I asked again.

"I thought you knew, Jessica. Peter is down in Georgia working on a photographic essay about the Okefenokee Swamp." She spoke with pride. "You can get an absence from school for special educational and cultural projects, you see, and all Peter's teachers agreed that he was a strong enough student to be able to make up two weeks' worth of work. He's been studying hard to get ahead."

"You mean he's going to be gone for two weeks!"

"Yes," she said. "So independent!" This last was a little defensive since even Mrs. F. realized that everybody in the neighborhood thought she had babied Peter too much. "My goodness," she interrupted herself. "Isn't that a police car pulling up to your house?"

"I'd better go." I ran to the house and threw open the back door. "Mom!" I said. "It's the police!"

Mom and Manuela looked up at me, startled. At the same time, I heard the front door bell ring. Manuela rose hastily. "I go," she said simply.

"Take the door that goes to the garage," I said. "That way you won't have to run into them."

Manuela's English was shaky and I wasn't sure she understood what I was saying so I opened the door to the garage myself and also pressed the button to open the garage door for her. Meanwhile, Mom went in to meet the police. By the time I got into the living room, two policemen were sitting heavily on the couch. One had a spiral-bound notebook balanced on one knee.

"You say he's gone out jogging?" said the skinny blond policeman.

"That's right," Mom said. "He just left, so it may be a while before he returns. Of course, you're welcome to wait here."

"Maybe we can just ask you a few questions while we're here," said the plump policeman. His neck was red and it looked as if his collar were too tight. "We're trying to trace Angela Nicholson's car, but meanwhile we're asking everyone who knew her if they have any clue as to where she could be. Did she ever mention that she might be going away somewhere? Did she have any friends or acquaintances that seemed suspicious in any way to you?"

"I'm afraid I didn't know her very well, officer," Mom said.

"I knew her," I said. "I mean, I *know* her." I felt terrible that we were already speaking of Angela in the past tense. "I used to ride to lunch with her every day. She never mentioned anything about going away to me. Of course, I haven't seen her much just lately."

"Why was that, Miss?" asked the thin officer.

"Well," I said, "for a while there she was going to lunch with Wyndy every day and then . . . then she just quit."

"Lovers' quarrel?" suggested the fat officer, smirking.

"Oh, no," I said. "Nothing like that. I guess they just started seeing a little less of each other, that's all."

"The officers will want to ask Wyndy himself about all this," Mom said, her eyes suggesting that I shut up.

"Oh, right!" I said promptly. "I don't really know that much about it." I sat there uncomfortably for a while looking at their guns in black holsters on their hips.

I got up. "Maybe I'd better go get started on my homework," I said awkwardly. "You don't really think something has happened to her, do you?"

"We hope not. At this point we're just investigating, ma'am," said the plump officer.

Not long after I went to my room, I heard Wyndy coming in the front door. He had cut his jogging short after all. Maybe he had seen the police car. From my room I couldn't hear what was said while they were interviewing him, but Mom sat in on the interview and it was clear she didn't like the way it went because the minute the police left she called Dad at work and he came home.

After Dad got home, we all converged at the kitchen table for a conference. Wyndy was still in his jogging clothes but had thrown a towel around his neck. "You didn't have to come home, Richard," he was telling Dad. "The police can't really think I killed Angela."

"I didn't like the drift of their questions," Mom said. "I didn't like it at all."

"Well, I *didn't* kill Angela," said Wyndy, looking mildly amused, "so there's nothing to worry about."

Dad ignored him. "We'd better call Sally," he said, looking grave. "We need a lawyer to sit in the next time the police question Wyndy."

Mom jumped up. "I'm going to call her right now. I'll phone from the bedroom."

We sat at the table in somber silence until Mom returned. "I couldn't get her," she said. "She's gone off somewhere and her friend doesn't expect her back for weeks. But I did reach someone very helpful at Sarto Motors International in New York. They're going to have their legal department call me tomorrow with the names of some suitable lawyers."

Wyndy moved restlessly in his seat. "I think you're taking this too seriously," he said.

"Wyndy," Mom said, "when the police take your passport, believe me, they are not fooling around."

"Do you really think Wyndy is a suspect, Mom?" I asked.

"Why, no, sugar. Not a serious suspect. After all, he hasn't even seen Angela since Friday afternoon at school. But naturally it's their business to question everybody."

Dad added, "And it's our business to take steps to protect ourselves."

"I think I'll call Molly," Mom said, "and ask her to check out prominent criminal attorneys in our state. She may have some good ideas."

While Mom called Aunt Molly, I sat silently at the table wishing that Wyndy had told the police he had been out with Angela late Friday night. Could I have been wrong about seeing her in the Hirondelle? Could the girl in the car have been Ashley in a platinum wig? Nah. Not likely. Why would Ashley want to wear a platinum wig?

When Mom got through to Aunt Molly, Mom, Dad and Wyndy ensconced themselves at the kitchen phone with a yellow legal pad and began the process of becoming very well informed about prominent criminal lawyers in North Carolina. I got up and wandered listlessly around the house.

The mail was still sitting on the little round table in the entry hall. I leafed through it aimlessly. There were no foreign stamps, but there was one very messed-up letter that looked as if it had been torn up and spit out by the post office's sorting machines. I picked it up and saw that it was addressed to me. It had a postmark that was several weeks old.

I tore it open and to my astonishment a check fell out. I held it up to the light and looked at it closely. It was a check for one hundred dollars from *Goblin Magazine*! I fished the letter out of the mutilated envelope. It was hardly in better shape than the envelope, but I could make out what it said. I had won third prize in *Goblin Magazine*'s horror story contest! My story would be appearing in the December issue.

I held the letter in stiff fingers. The December issue? We were already well into November. The December issue might already be on the stands. It might, at least, be about to come on the stands. In other circumstances, I would have been dancing into the kitchen waving the check with shouts of joy. I had won! But it hit me with a very unpleasant thud that I could hardly announce my victory without everyone in the family wanting to run right out and buy a copy of the magazine in order to read my story. They would recognize right away the nasty sketch of Wyndy. I hadn't made the slightest effort to disguise him.

I realized my situation was something worse than awkward—it was horrible. Not only had my feelings about Wyndy changed completely since I had written the story, but on top of that it was definitely not the kind of story to drop into a police investigation. After all, if it had been good enough to win *Goblin Magazine*'s third prize, it might just be good enough to convince the police that Wyndy was the sinister foreigner I had portrayed, the bloodsucking one who killed young girls.

I tucked the check back into the envelope and quietly tiptoed back to my room. Opening my bureau drawer, I hid it under a stack of clean underwear. I would just let this whole matter blow over quietly. How many people were regular readers of *Goblin Magazine* anyway?

Chapter Ten

The next morning when I walked into the crowded lobby at school, I got a dreadful shock. A card table had been put up in the corner of the lobby and it was piled high with magazines. On the wall behind the table was a poster that said, Goblin Magazine—$3. Read the *Prizewinning Horror Story* by a *Senior High Student*. A Fund-raising Project of the Literary Club.

I managed to work my way through the crowd and over to the table. Smiling brightly at the girl with the stringy hair who was selling the magazines, I asked, "How many of those do you have left?"

She looked around the table, checked out a cardboard box under the table and said, "About fifty."

"I'll take them all," I said. "Will you take an I.O.U.?"

"No credit," she said, looking at me hostilely.

As I crept away, I saw that Marian was eyeing me. A moment later, I saw her go over to the table and buy a copy of the magazine.

I bumped into Karen. "Karen," I said, grabbing hold of her

desperately. "Can I borrow a hundred and fifty dollars right away?"

She didn't seem to hear me. Her eyes were filled with tears. "Oh, Jess, isn't it awful about poor Angela! I just can't believe it! The police were actually over at our house yesterday."

"Our house, too," I said, suddenly sobered. "It's terrible. I just keep hoping she'll come back home."

"Tony locked himself in his room all evening he was so upset," Karen said. "Somebody that we all know! It's horrible."

"Wyndy seems to think she's okay. He thinks maybe she took it in her head to go skiing or something and just didn't tell anybody."

"Poor Wyndy," she moaned. "How awful it must be for him. It makes me feel sick to my stomach. It's terrible."

The bell rang and Karen and I both nearly jumped out of our skins. As we joined the crowd trying to squeeze into the hallway, I noticed with a sinking heart that the stack of magazines on the card table had grown noticeably smaller.

Angela's disappearance was all people could talk about that day. After school, Wyndy and I drove home almost in silence. Obviously he too had been affected by the general atmosphere of mourning. As we pulled up in the driveway at home he reached over carelessly and ruffled my hair. "Cheer up, Jess," he said. "It's not as bad as all that. She'll turn up. You'll see."

I looked over at him, a cold feeling in my stomach. I wanted to ask him why he hadn't told the police that he had seen Angela Friday night but every time I started to ask, my throat felt so tight I couldn't speak. I got out of the car slowly and went inside.

I was sure Wyndy knew more about Angela's disappearance than he was telling. Maybe she had even told him where she was going. But if she had, I didn't understand why he was keeping it a secret. It worried me that he concealed the Friday night date from the police. He just didn't understand that everybody should respect the law. Obviously, somebody should have read him *The Policeman Is Our Friend* during his formative years, but it was too late now. He was the way he was and there was no changing him. What mattered to Wyndy, I knew, was not the law but the network of people who were bound to him personally—the people who worked for his father, his friends, his family—the people, he would have said, that you could count on. Possibly he didn't even realize that keeping things from the police could be a serious offense. I was worried that he might be getting into more trouble than he realized. On top of that I was worried that Wyndy would get hold of a copy of *Goblin Magazine* and wouldn't trust me anymore. How could I blame him? I felt terrible.

As soon as we got inside, I went straight to my room, fished the prize check out of my underwear drawer and set out immediately for our neighborhood branch bank to cash it. I needed the money now. I was going to buy up a lot of *Goblin Magazines*.

First thing the next morning, as soon as I got to school, I rushed into the lobby and bought the modest pile of magazines the Literary Club had left. I would never have dreamed there were so many kids who read horror stories. Under normal circumstances my author's heart would have been swelling with pride that so many people were willing to plunk down three hard-earned dollars to read my work, but under these circumstances, I felt sick to my stomach.

Mac sidled up to me after homeroom. "Gosh, Jess, I read your story. Nice going! Say, is it all true?"

"You know that people don't really turn into vampires! It's just a story."

"Heh, heh, sure I know that," he said. "But like I just happened to notice that it seemed to be based on real life, you see what I mean?" He lowered his voice. "Couldn't help seeing that the vampire is just like that Sarto guy, what's-his-name. I mean, looks like him, dresses like him, talks like him."

"But the story is just for fun! It doesn't mean anything! I just wrote it when I got so mad at Wyndy for using up all the hot water."

"Oh! Like that, huh? You know my sister uses up all the hot water, too. And you should see the way she ties up the telephone. It's enough to drive a fella bonkers. Well, it was a heck of a story anyway. Scared me to death."

"Thank you," I said in a small voice. I had been able to explain things to Mac. That was something. But how could I explain the story to every single person who bought a copy of the magazine?

At lunchtime, I met Wyndy at the Hirondelle with my guilty conscience written all over my face. I felt terrible. Wyndy didn't seem to be in good spirits, either. At lunch he just picked at his food, which was not like him.

"Do you feel okay?" I asked anxiously. "You've hardly eaten a thing."

He broke a French fry in half and looked at it as if he were a disgruntled food inspector. "I think some of the kids think I did away with Angela."

"What makes you think that?"

"Well, it's like this. A bunch of people will be standing around talking and when I get close—they stop. That kind of thing. It's hard to explain but you should see the looks I'm getting! I know you're thinking it's my imagination, but it's not."

He tossed the broken fry back onto the plate. "Ashley looked as if she was afraid I was going to strangle her or something. I swear to you, I walked up and she turned white and started inching her way backward. She darned near tripped over a chair."

"Oh, dear."

"*You* don't think I murdered Angela, do you?"

"No, certainly not," I said hastily. "Never."

"It's pretty bad, I can tell you. I'm not the sensitive type, but it's a bit thick to have the whole junior class practically passing out when you get close to them. If the police didn't have my passport I'd be out of this place tomorrow. Why should I hang around and put up with all this stuff?" He threw his scarcely touched sandwich and fries back in their paper sack, crumbled up the bag with a fierce gesture and threw it with unerring aim into the trash bin that stood in front of the elm tree. He immediately revved up the engine when I got back in the car. We didn't say a word all the way back to school.

When we reached the school parking lot, he didn't even switch off the engine. "Take the bus home this afternoon, Jess," he said. "I'm cutting out."

He drove out of the lot with a roar. I noticed a number of people's eyes followed the car as he drove away. Marian and Karen were standing with Kim and her friends near Kim's big old Plymouth. I didn't have to ask what they were talking about. I knew. I stalked over to them, the gravel of the parking lot crunching under my angry steps.

"Hey, Jessica," Marian said as I approached. "I read your story. Congratulations on winning third prize."

"Marian says it's a super story," Karen put in.

"It *was* a good story," I said. "And that's all it was, a story. I certainly would think that everybody at Senior High is old enough to tell the difference between fact and fiction."

"Well," said Marian, "you know what people say: Where there's smoke there's fire."

"Honestly!" I said. "Do you think that if I believed Wyndy were a murderer I would go on riding everywhere with him? It's the most ridiculous idea in the world."

"He did just drive off in a hurry just now," said Marian with a smug look. "*Something* must be bothering him if he's going to cut afternoon classes."

"You are what's bothering him, Marian," I said hotly. "You and all the other gossiping idiots. It'd be enough to drive anybody crazy to have people standing around saying they're a murderer. You need a new hobby, Marian Beasley. What's the matter with you? All you do is stand around talking about other people. It's disgusting!"

"Well!" huffed Marian. "What's *your* problem? You're awfully worried about Wyndham all of a sudden, aren't you?"

I turned on my heel and stormed out of the parking lot. It was true. I *was* worried about Wyndy. I hated to see him getting hurt. It made it worse that I was the one who had helped put him in the fix he was in. I felt like a traitor. When I thought about how unhappy he was, I felt like bursting into tears.

After school I took the bus home. As I got on the bus several people complimented me on my horror story. Three of them asked me if it were based on fact and Tina Yelverton asked me, with wide eyes, why it was that I wasn't riding home with Wyndy this afternoon the way I usually did. I felt like standing up in the aisle and screaming that Wyndy was not a murderer. To all inquirers I explained that Wyndy had a few errands to run so I had taken the bus home. To a couple of people I pointed out the difference between truth and fiction, adding that vampires and werewolves did not, in fact, attend Senior High.

There was no sign of Wyndy or the Hirondelle when I got off the bus at home, so when I went in the house I asked Mom if she had seen him. "He got in a few minutes ago," she said, "but he went off with Tony."

A little later I was sitting in the living room trying without much success to read the next weeks' history assignment, when Wyndy came back. He was dangling a tennis racket in his hand and had a copy of *Goblin Magazine* tucked under his arm. His dark eyes were contemptuous and there was a white rigidity around his mouth and nose. He must have looked at me a full minute before he turned without saying a word and went back to his room. A few minutes later I heard the sound of the shower.

Mom peeked out of the kitchen. "Did I hear Wyndy come in?"

"Yes," I said.

"I'm glad he went out with Tony," said Mom. "He seems to be awfully upset about Angela. It's a terrible thing. We're all upset, of course, but it's worse for Wyndy."

"Yes," I said.

She sighed and went back to the kitchen.

I wished I could explain to Wyndy. But what could I say? I really had done a rotten thing and there was no possible excuse for it. My head felt tight like a stretched rubber band. I finally went into my room and lay down. I wondered if he would tell Mom and Dad about my story. But I realized he wouldn't. It would have been completely unlike him to give me away. He would have said it was beneath him.

After a while I heard Wyndy's bedroom door open. Then, outside, I heard the Hirondelle roar and take off.

At first my mind was too filled with the memory of the expression on Wyndy's face for me to be able to concentrate on anything else. Finally I decided I would write to Audrey and tell her all about what had happened. It would take a long time to fill her in but it would be worth it. She would see my point of view. Also, she would be on my side, no matter how much of a mess I had made of things. I put a fresh sheet of paper into my typewriter. I certainly wished Audrey were with me right then to cheer me up. I took out my calendar and counted up the days until Thanksgiving when she would be home. Then I started the letter. When I'd finished, it completely and satisfactorily explained that I hadn't really done anything so terrible after all and I began to feel a little better.

I began groping around in my desk drawer for a stamp and came up with twelve return address labels, some rubber bands, a package of staples, a dried-up marking pen, an address book, and the lanyard I'd made at camp when I was eight. No stamps. I would just nip into Wyndy's room and get a stamp. I knew he had a whole roll of them because he had given me one the last time I wrote Audrey. I would borrow a stamp, I decided. Then I would walk down to the mailbox and mail my letter.

The door of his room had been left open. I went in and pulled the top desk drawer open but didn't at first see the stamps. Then I rustled around among the odds and ends in the drawer. Suddenly I saw something glittering. I pushed a few papers aside so I could see it clearly. It was Angela's topaz ring, the one she wore on her thumb. I picked it up and held it in my hand. The stone glittered like a living thing.

I heard a sound at the door and wheeled around, still clutching the ring. Wyndy was leaning against the door frame, his arms folded over his chest.

"Wyndy!" I said hoarsely. "Where did you get Angela's ring?"

"Took it from her lifeless finger, of course."

"Very funny."

"Thank you. It does great things for my sense of humor to find out that everyone thinks I'm a murderer."

"You know that I don't think you're a murderer."

"I do? Funny, the story in that magazine gave me the idea that you did. And of course when I come in and find you searching my desk, your face as white as your shirt, I couldn't help jumping to the conclusion that you were looking for some evidence against me. Well, you've found it. Happy?"

I sat down in the desk chair. My knees were feeling a bit too weak to hold me up.

"Silly idiot!" I said. "I know you didn't kill Angela. I never thought that for a minute." I took a deep breath. "I'm sorry about the story, Wyndy. I really am. I wrote it ages ago when I was mad at you for using up all the hot water. How could I know it would win the dumb prize and that the Literary Club would be selling it all over the school? I'm sorry, I'm sorry, I'm sorry. What else can I say?" I looked at him helplessly. I couldn't tell anything about what he was thinking from his expression. "Where is Angela?" I asked. "I know you saw her Friday night because I saw you at Ronnie's together. She told you then what she was up to, didn't she?"

He looked at me from under his black eyelashes. "You didn't tell the police that you saw me that night with Angela?"

"Well, no," I said uncomfortably.

"I thought you were such a big fan of the police's."

I didn't have anything to say to that. It was just another example of how my principles tended to crumble when Wyndy was around.

"Could it be that you're a bigger fan of mine than of theirs?" he said softly, starting to smile.

When I saw that he had started smiling at me in the old way, I immediately and irrationally felt as if everything were going to be all right. Seeing that smile was like watching the sun play on my grandmother's cut glass sugar bowl. It was a dazzling display of brightness. I felt a hundred percent better. He was forgiving me for that rotten story.

He took the ring from my hand, put it back in the drawer and pushed the drawer closed again.

"She gave you that ring when she went away, didn't she?" I asked.

"Yup. She flagged me down Friday night when I was taking Ashley home. They live on the same block, you see. So I drove her to Ronnie's and we got coffee. I figured she was just going to cry on my shoulder some more. Angela was always telling me about her troubles with her parents. But she surprised me. Told me she was leaving home for good. I tried to talk her out of it, naturally, but it was no go. Then she sort of pressed the ring on me. Said she wanted me to have something to remember her by. Angela can get pretty soupy. There wasn't anything I could do but take it."

"So where is she now?"

"Can't tell you that. Promised I'd keep it a secret."

"But if Angela could see what's been going on since she left, she wouldn't expect you to stick by the promise. Everybody's going crazy! Think of her poor parents! Think about how they must feel!"

"A little shock will do 'em good," he said. "They've been ignoring Angela for years. So she decided to ignore them for a change, I guess."

"But they're crazy out of their minds worrying about her! And what about the police? They're looking for her all over the state when all the time you know just where she is."

"I promised her I wouldn't tell," he said stubbornly.

"Do you want to end up in jail?"

We looked at each other for a moment. I had never noticed before what a firm chin Wyndy had. I heard the front door open. "That's Dad," I said. "I'm going to tell him."

"Don't do that," he said.

"Then you tell him."

There was a brief silence. Then finally he said, "All right. I'll tell him." He tugged at his earlobe uncomfortably. It was the only ungraceful gesture I had ever seen him make. "I've been thinking for a while now that it was going to come to this," he confessed. "This whole thing has gotten out of hand."

I let out my breath in a rush and closed my eyes in relief as he turned and went to find Dad.

After he had gone, I looked at the letter to Audrey that was lying on top of Wyndy's desk. It seemed like ancient history now. I picked it up and tore it in half. I would have to explain everything to her at Thanksgiving instead. Things were happening too fast now for me to keep her up-to-date.

After Dad had heard Wyndy's story, he didn't wait to eat dinner. He called the lawyer and told him to meet the two of them at the police station, then he drove Wyndy right over there.

It was some time before they got back and when they did they were in no mood to talk. Wyndy went straight to his room. Dad steadfastly ate his cold roast beef in silence, saying that the story wasn't his to tell.

I got the whole story later that night from Karen, who'd heard it all when Peter's mother was down at the Harper's house having hysterics. It turned out that Peter wasn't in the Okefenokee Swamp after all. He and Angela had run away to get married! But evidently the idea of getting married had seemed less and less attractive to them as they traveled south from one bleak gas station to another and they had chickened out. Karen told me that when the police car arrived to pick them up they were in a motel room arguing about what to do next. They had run out of both money and nerve in Athens, Georgia, and once the police knew in which direction they should be looking, they had no trouble at all finding Angela's Trans Am.

"What idiots," I said to Karen, curling up at the foot of her bed that evening. "What did they expect to do for money?"

"Peter was thinking of supporting them by selling his photos. They had also talked about moving in with Peter's parents after they got married."

"What a laugh! Mrs. Fields can't stand Angela."

"I'm not too clear on the details," Karen said. "When Mrs. Fields was telling my mom about it I couldn't always understand what she was saying. She was talking awfully loud, but she was so upset it got kind of garbled. I think Mr. Fields and Mr. Nicholson are driving down in separate cars to fetch them."

"In a way Peter and Angela are a perfect match," I said. "They're certainly the two silliest people I know."

"I thought you kind of liked Peter."

"I outgrew him," I said loftily.

"What I can't believe," said Karen, "is that Wyndy knew it all the time. Why didn't he tell anybody?"

"Angela swore him to secrecy. That's all."

"Still!" said Karen. "When you think of how upset we all were! Thinking Angela was dead and all that. Mrs. Fields says her only comfort is that Angela's Dad says he's going to send Angela away to a convent school with walls nine feet high."

"So she blames Angela for the whole thing."

"Naturally," said Karen.

"Mrs. Fields is an idiot," I said. "Peter was the one chasing Angela. Even I could see that."

Chapter Eleven

For school the next day, I wore another of my new outfits, a black turtleneck sweater, snug black wool-knit pants and a vivid fuchsia cardigan slung round my shoulders like a cape, precisely what the well-dressed cat burglar should wear.

Mom paused a moment, spatula in hand as she looked me up and down. "I like that one," she said. "It's really you. Where did you get it?"

I sat down contentedly to my Rice Krispies. "I told you, Mom. At this cut-rate warehouse in Raleigh. I got a ride over that day Wyndy took the car to be checked."

"I know, but what was the name of the warehouse, Jess? You got such terrific bargains, I think I ought to go myself and take a look at what they've got."

"It's called Adolpho's," I said, pouring out my cereal.

Under the table, Wyndy kicked me. I looked up at him in alarm.

"You must have the name wrong," Mom said. "Adolpho's is the name of an Italian couturier. I know because Ann Mattingly got a dress at their Raleigh branch for Sara's debut. It cost the earth.''

"I guess I must have forgotten the name of the place," I said quickly.

"I wish you would go look for your receipt and get the right name for me, dear. I need a really drop-dead special dress for the Momeyers' Christmas party and I don't want to have to spend a fortune on it.''

"It's no use, Mom," I said, thinking fast. "I bought all this stuff at their going out of business sale.''

"You mean they've gone out of business?"

"That's right.''

Wyndy shot me an approving look.

"Just as well, Susan," commented Dad from behind the paper. "I, for one, am not ready for a whole new you.''

I gulped a few more mouthfuls of cereal. "We'd better run," I said. Wyndy and I lost no time ducking out of the kitchen before there were any more awkward questions. But when we were in the car and driving safely away I could speak freely. "Wyndy!" I screeched. "How could you *do* that to me? How could you let me think all those things came from some cut-rate warehouse? Mom will kill me if she finds out you bought all those clothes at that Adolpho's place." I thought a minute. "She'll kill you, too.''

"So how's she going to find out? You did a pretty good job of thinking on your feet in there.''

"You know I can't take a present like that from you!"

"You don't have much choice, do you? Not at this point. What are you going to do? Burn them?"

"Why did you do such a crazy thing?"

"I thought it would be fun. Mostly it was, too, except that I got some pretty funny looks at Adolpho's.''

I covered my eyes with my hands. "It is not proper. It's not right for boys to give clothes to girls. Mom would die.''

"Well, you told me I could get the clothes. So I ran a little over budget, so what?''

I groaned.

"You have a nerve to be taking a high-and-mighty tone with me," he said, flashing his white teeth, "after writing that story about me. At least I didn't have the entire school thinking you committed murder."

He had a point. I had to admit it. I sat for a moment feeling chastened.

"I really appreciate your forgiving me for that," I said finally in a small voice.

Silently, he reached over and ruffled my hair.

At school, nobody could talk about anything else except Angela's and Peter's elopement. The full details had spread like wildfire thanks to the way Mrs. Fields had gone all over the place complaining to everybody she knew. At school, Tony Harper was spreading the story of how Angela had pledged Wyndy to secrecy and the general feeling seemed to be that he had behaved chivalrously, if not wisely. At lunchtime over sandwiches at Ronnie's, Wyndy reported that people were falling all over themselves being friendly to him. "This is getting to be popular the hard way," he said with some bitterness.

"People were awfully jumpy there for a while," I said. "Nobody was thinking too clearly. You shouldn't take it so seriously."

I noticed that his hair had fallen down into his face and he hadn't bothered to comb it. I liked it that way. It made me want to run my fingers through it, though I knew that would have horrified him.

He looked at me, his eyes troubled. "I was afraid it was going to be kind of a blow to you when you found out that Peter had run off with Angela."

"Oh, no," I said. "I should have seen it coming. I knew Peter was gaga about her and they seemed to be made for each other when you think about it. As I told Karen—they're the two silliest people I know." Then I was afraid I had gone too far. After all, Wyndy had dated Angela for ages. Maybe he didn't think she was silly at all. I added hastily, "It must have been an awful shock to *you*. What on earth did you say when Angela told you what she was up to?"

"I tried to knock a little sense into her head just the way anybody would, but it was hopeless. She had this idea she was going to live happily ever after. So I wished her luck. What could I do? You can't go living other people's lives for them."

"Too true. Though in Peter's case the temptation is a big one since he makes such a mess of living his own life. He can't do anything right."

"Hey, I thought you liked him."

"Temporary insanity. I've realized for a long time I like a different sort of boy. You know, somebody who knows what they're doing, somebody with a sense of humor."

He bit into his sandwich thoughtfully. "Funny thing, I've had something happen kind of like that. I used to think I liked skinny blondes but lately I've got this taste for small brunettes."

"How interesting," I said. "The thing is when you really find a person that you really like then you realize that a lot of other things just are not very important."

"Absolutely," he said. His eyes took on their triangular look as he laughed inside. "You think either of us will ever find somebody like that?"

That was when I lost my temper and whopped him on the arm with my fist. He caught both my hands in his, leaned over the gearshift and kissed me. Then he kissed me on the nose; after that we had another kiss that was very nice, and the upshot was we were late getting back from lunch and we both drew detention—but it was worth it.

Wyndy and I kept our new feelings toward each other a secret from Mom and Dad. It was not only because a person naturally wants some privacy, but also because I remembered how panicky Mom had been that day in the airport and I was afraid if she sensed how close Wyndy and I were getting to be these days she would have that garage turned into an apartment for him as quick as a wink and Wyndy would be sent to live there.

We saved our snuggling for the parking lot at Ronnie's. Luckily, we were still having warm weather in the middle of the day so we could sit in the car to eat. Not that the Hirondelle was ideal for snuggling. The bucket seats and the gearshift presented a problem. Still, it was nice to be together, I thought as we sat in the car a few days later. Wyndy was nuzzling my ear. "When you go to type the announcements this afternoon I think you'll find one that you like," he murmured after a suitable interval.

I sat bolt upright. "Tell me. Is it something about senior privileges?"

"Don't you want to be surprised?"

"Tell me!"

"Okay. Tony says the student council voted to have a referendum on senior privileges. Everybody will get to vote on whether to have them or not."

"Oh, this is fantastic! I can't believe it's happened so soon."

He grinned. "So you're sure you're going to win?"

I snuggled back up against him. "Oh, I think we'll win. People are such sheep. I'll just keep putting my thoughts for the day in every day's bulletin."

"You are a dangerous woman, Jess."

"Thank you," I said. We kissed again. With only forty minutes for lunch a person could lose a lot of weight that way.

When we got home from school, I was alarmed to see a letter with a foreign stamp on the entry hall table. It was not Ferreti's handwriting this time and it was a totally different envelope, too. A big, heavy, grand-looking envelope. I couldn't read the spiky handwriting, but I didn't have to. It had to be from Giovanni. I remembered Wyndy saying that his handwriting on an envelope meant trouble.

Wyndy stayed in his room a long time. When he came out, his lips were set and he was in his jogging clothes. "Want to run?" he asked me.

"Sure, just a minute." I ran to my room and threw on some jeans as fast as I could. A few minutes later we were jogging down the street. "News from home?" I inquired.

"Yes," he said.

When we got to the park, Wyndy stopped and collapsed on a bench. I knew he had to be really upset because that was bad training. I sat down beside him, panting.

"Do you want to talk about it?" I said.

"Giovanni's out of Montesano," he said. "He and Sally are back together. They're trying to work things out."

"That's good," I said doubtfully. From my point of view I was not sure whether it was good or not. "Does he want you to come live with them?"

"He doesn't come right out and say so."

"What does he say?"

"Not much. It's a very Italian letter—lots of emotion and not much news."

"Do you want to go?"

"No way. There's a fifty-fifty chance it'll all go bust with a lot of screaming and broken bottles. I don't need the grief."

"So stay here."

"It's not that easy. The thing is, I've done without Giovanni for years now. I don't need him anymore."

"Well, there it is, then."

"The question is, does *he* need *me*?"

"Probably it's better for them to work things out just the two of them without the complication of having you around," I said.

"Is that an impartial opinion?"

"Probably not."

"Why should I tear my life apart just on the off chance he's going to be able to stay sober?"

"You could wait till the end of the school year and see if it works out and *then* you could go home."

"I guess so. Do you think that's what I ought to do?"

"I don't know," I said, honestly.

"I'll probably feel awful no matter what I do."

"Why should you feel awful? It's not your fault your father's life is all messed up."

"It's not as if I could make everything work out for him by going back."

"That's right."

"We ought not to be sitting here when we're all hot. It's rotten training."

I got up obediently and we began trotting slowly through the park. "I don't want to go," he said. I immediately began to feel more cheerful. I knew Wyndy pretty well and I couldn't really see him doing something he didn't want to do. "I'll bet spring is pretty around here," he said.

"Beautiful. Daffodils, clouds of flowers, drifts of dogwood, blue skies."

"Organdies, linens, straw hats," he countered. He shot me a calculating look. "When did you say you get your next clothes allowance?"

I groaned. "Look, Wyndy, I'm going to have to buy my own clothes."

"I could just go along as a technical adviser."

"I guess that would be all right. But I have to pay for them all myself. My clothing budget may not be that big, but I've got to manage on it."

"Sure."

"As long as that's settled," I said. I hoped my voice was filled with confidence, but underneath I felt uncertain that it was all as settled as I had claimed. I had the feeling that nothing was ever going to be completely settled as long as Wyndy was around. But to my surprise, instead of worrying about it the way I usually do about the idea of anything new, I felt a pleasant tingle of anticipation. New adventures ahead. Right around that next corner, where I could just now make out Mrs. Henniker's black cat playing with an unwinding ball of string.

QUANTITY	BOOK #	ISBN #	TITLE	AUTHOR	PRICE
☐	129	06129-3	The Ghost of Gamma Rho	Elaine Harper	$1.95
☐	130	06130-7	Nightshade	Jesse Osborne	1.95
☐	131	06131-5	Waiting for Amanda	Cheryl Zach	1.95
☐	132	06132-3	The Candy Papers	Helen Cavanagh	1.95
☐	133	06133-1	Manhattan Melody	Marilyn Youngblood	1.95
☐	134	06134-X	Killebrew's Daughter	Janice Harrell	1.95
☐	135	06135-8	Bid for Romance	Dorothy Francis	1.95
☐	136	06136-6	The Shadow Knows	Becky Stewart	1.95
☐	137	06137-4	Lover's Lake	Elaine Harper	1.95
☐	138	06138-2	In the Money	Beverly Sommers	1.95
☐	139	06139-0	Breaking Away	Josephine Wunsch	1.95
☐	140	06140-4	What I Know About Boys	McClure Jones	1.95
☐	141	06141-2	I Love You More Than Chocolate	Frances Hurley Grimes	1.95
☐	142	06142-0	The Wilder Special	Rose Bayner	1.95
☐	143	06143-9	Hungarian Rhapsody	Marilyn Youngblood	1.95
☐	144	06144-7	Country Boy	Joyce McGill	1.95
☐	145	06145-5	Janine	Elaine Harper	1.95
☐	146	06146-3	Call Back Yesterday	Doreen Owens Malek	1.95
☐	147	06147-1	Why Me?	Beverly Sommers	1.95
☐	149	06149-8	Off the Hook	Rose Bayner	1.95
☐	150	06150-1	The Heartbreak of Haltom High	Dawn Kingsbury	1.95
☐	151	06151-X	Against the Odds	Andrea Marshall	1.95
☐	152	06152-8	On the Road Again	Miriam Morton	1.95
☐	159	06159-5	Sugar 'n' Spice	Janice Harrell	1.95
☐	160	06160-9	The Other Langley Girl	Joyce McGill	1.95

Your Order Total $ _____

☐ (Minimum 2 Book Order)
New York and Arizona residents
add appropriate sales tax $ _____

Postage and Handling   .75

I enclose   _____

Name_____

Address_____

City_____

State/Prov._____Zip/Postal Code_____

FL-RO-2